9780505513540

The Two Bands Met
In Bloody Collision!

The chariot overturned and shattered, sending one wheel flying and spilling both riders into the muck. Gerin ran forward to finish Viredorix, but the Trokmê lit rolling and rushed to meet him. "A fine thing will the skull of you be over my gate," he shouted, and then their blades joined with a clash of sparks and there was no more time for words.

Slashing and chopping, Viredorix surged forward, trying to overwhelm his smaller foe at the first onset. Gerin parried desperately; he would have been sliced in two had any of the Trokmê's cuts landed. When Viredorix's blade bit so deep into the edge of his shield that it stuck for a moment, the Fox seized the chance for a thrust of his own, but Viredorix knocked his questing point aside with a dagger in his left hand.

With a groan, Gerin went to one knee. Thinking him finished, the Trokmê loomed over him, eager to take his head. But Gerin was not yet done. His sword shot up and out with all the force of his body behind it, and its point tore out Viredorix's throat. Dark in the gloom, his lifeblood fountained forth as he fell, both hands clutching futilely at his neck.

WEREBLOOD

ERIK IVERSON

BELMONT TOWER BOOKS • NEW YORK CITY

A BELMONT TOWER BOOK

Published by

Tower Publications, Inc.
Two Park Avenue
New York, N.Y. 10016

chapter 1

"Duin, you're a damned fool if you think you can fight from horseback," said Drago the Bear, tossing a gnawed bone to his trencher.

Duin the Bold slammed his tankard down on the long table; ale slopped over the rim. "Fool, is it?" he shouted, his fair face reddening. "You're the fool, you thickskulled muckbrain!"

Drago stormed up with an oath, murder in his eyes, thick arms groping toward Duin. The slimmer man skipped back; his hand flashed to his swordhilt. Cries of anger and alarm rang through Castle Fox's great hall. Gerin the Fox, baron of Fox Keep, leaped to his feet. "Stop it!" he shouted, and the shout froze both angry men for a moment, giving their benchmates a chance to crowd between them. Drago sent one man flying with a shrug of his massive shoulders, but was brought up short by a grip not even his massive thews could break. The outlander Van of the Strong Arm grinned down at him. Almost a foot taller than the squat Bear, he was every bit as powerfully made, and no man in Castle Fox had yet seen his full strength exerted.

Gerin glowered at his fractious vassals, absolute

disgust plain in every line of his lean body. Both men grew shamefaced under his glare. Nothing would have pleased him more than breaking both their stupid heads; instead he lashed them with his voice, snapping, "I called you here to fight the Trokmoi, not each other. The woodsrunners will be a tough enough nut to crack without us squabbling among ourselves."

"Then let us fight them!" Duin exclaimed, but his blade was back in its scabbard. He went on, "This Dyaus-damned rain has cooped us up for ten days now. It's no wonder we're quarreling like so many snapping turtles in a pot. Turn us loose, lord Gerin!" To that even Drago rumbled agreement, and he was not alone.

The Fox shook his head. "If we try to cross the River Niffet in this weather, either current or storm will be sure to swamp us. When the sky clears, we move. Not before." Privately, Gerin was more worried than his liegemen, but he did not want them to see that. Since spring began he'd been sure the northern barbarians were planning to swarm south over the Niffet and ravage his holding, and had decided to strike first himself. But this downpour—worse than any he could recall in all his thirty years on the northern marches of the Empire of Elabon—had balked his plans. For ten days there had been no glimpse of sun, moons, or stars. Even the Niffet, a scant half mile away, was hard to spy. Too, rumor said the Trokmoi had a new wizard of great power. More than once the baron had seen fell lights dancing deep within the northern forests, and his ever-suspicious mind found it all too easy to blame the Trokmê mage for the rude weather.

6

Duin started a further protest, but saw the scar over Gerin's right eye go pale: a sure danger signal. The words stayed bottled in his throat. He made sheepish apologies to Drago, who frowned but, under Gerin's implacable gaze, nodded and clasped his hand.

As calm descended, the baron took a long pull at his own ale. The hour was late and he was tired, but he was not eager for bed; his chamber was on the second story, and the roof leaked. Siglorel Shelofas' son, when sober the best Elabonian wizard north of the High Kirs, had laid on a five-year calking spell only the summer before, but the old sot must have had a bad day, for water trickled through the roofing and collected in cold puddles on the upper story's floor. Spread rushes did all too little to soak it up.

Gerin plucked at his neat black beard and wished for carpets like those he had known in his younger days south of the mountains, when study was all he lived for and the barony the furthest thing from his mind. He remembered the fiasco that resulted when his exasperation drove him to try the book of spells he had brought north from the City of Elabon. History and natural lore had interested in him more than mage-craft; his studies at the Sorcerers' Collegium began late and, worse, were cut short after three months. An ambush laid by the Trokmoi had taken his father and elder brother, leaving him the unexpected master of Fox Keep. In the past eight years he had had little cause to try wizardry, and his skill was not large. Nor had age improved it: his incantation had raised nothing more than a cloud of stinking black smoke and the hackles of all his vassals. He counted

7

himself lucky; amateur wizards who played with forces stronger than they could control often met unpleasant ends.

A bit of drunken song made him look up. Duin and Drago were sitting with their arms round each other's shoulders, boasting of the havoc they would wreak among the Trokmoi when the cursed weather finally cleared. The baron was relieved; they were two of his stoutest fighting men. He drained his mug, rose to receive the salutes of his vassals and, head buzzing slightly, climbed the soot-grimed oak stairway leading to his bed-chamber. His last waking thought was a prayer to Dyaus for fair weather so he could add another chapter to the vengeance he was taking on the bar-barians . . .

A horn cried danger from the watchtower, tumbling him from his bed with the least ceremony imaginable. He cursed the bronzen clangor as he stumbled to a window. "If that overeager lackwit up there is tootling for his amusement," he mut-tered to himself, "I'll have his ears." But the scar over his eye was throbbing and his fingers were nervous in his beard; if the Trokmoi had found some way to cross the Niffet in the rain, there was no telling how much damage they could do.

The window was only a north-facing slit, intend-ed more for arrow fire than sight, but what it showed was enough. Jabbing forks of lightning revealed hand after hand of Trokmoi, all busily searching for something to carry off or, failing that, to burn. The wind blew snatches of their lilting speech to his ears.

"May the gods fry you, Viredorix, you tricky

8

bastard, and your pet wizard too," Gerin growled, wondering how the Trokmê chieftain had managed to get so many men across the river so quickly. Then he raised his eyes further and saw the bridge bulking impossibly huge over the Niffet.

It was plainly sorcerous, a silvery band of light leading from the northern woods into Gerin's holding, and it had not been there when the baron went to his rest a few hours before. Even as he watched, Trokmê nobles poured over it in their chariots, their retainers loping beside them. Once long ago, it seemed, he had read something of such spans; he could not recall where or when, but the half-memory sent a pang of fear icing up his spine.

No time for thought now. He hurled himself into trousers and hobnailed sandals, buckled on his sword, and rushed down dim-lit passageway and creaking stair to the great hall, where his lesser barons had hung their corselets when they arrived. The gleam of ruddy bronze in the torchlight was a delightsome thing to see, but now the hall was a swearing jumble of men donning metal-faced leather cuirasses and kilts, strapping on greaves, jamming pot-shaped helms onto their heads, and fouling each other as they waved spears in the air. Like Gerin, most had dark hair and eyes and skin that took the sun well, but a few freckled faces and light beards told of northern blood—Duin, for one, was fair as any Trokmê.

"Ho, Captain!" boomed Van of the Strong Arm. "Thought you'd never get here!"

Even in the rowdy crew Gerin led, Van stood out. Taller than the Fox's six feet by as many inches, he was broad enough not to look his height. A sword-cut creased his nose, wandered

9

over his cheek, and disappeared into the sun-colored mat of beard covering most of his face. Little hellish lights were flickering in his blue eyes.

His gear was as remarkable as his person, for his back-and-breast was cast of two solid pieces of bronze, and not even the Emperor had a finer one. Unlike the businesslike helmets his comrades wore, Van's was a fantastic affair with a scarlet horsehair plume nodding above his head and leather cheekpieces to protect his face. Looking more war-god than man, the outlander shook a spear like a young tree.

If his tale was true, he had been trying to cross the forests of the Trokmoi from north to south, and had all but done it until he fell foul of Viredorix's clan. But he had escaped them too, and had enough left in his giant frame to swim the Niffet, towing his precious armor behind him on a makeshift raft. His strength, bluff good humor, and wide-ranging fund of stories (told in the forest tongue until he learned Elabonian) won him a home at Fox Keep for as long as he wanted to stay. But when Gerin asked him his homeland he politely declined to answer. The Fox had not asked twice; if Van did not want to talk of that, it was his affair. That had been only two years ago, Gerin thought with a twinge of surprise; it was hard to recall what it had been like without his burly friend at his side.

The Fox's own armor was of the plainest, its leather much-patched, its plates battered and nicked. Patches and all, though, the leather was firm and supple, and every plate was sound. To Gerin's way of thinking, the figure he cut on the field was far less important than keeping himself alive and putting a quick end to his foes.

The warriors wallowed through thick mud to the stables. It squelched underfoot, trying to suck their sandals and boots into its cold slimy mouth. Inside the stables chaos was compounded, with boys trying to hitch unwilling horses to their masters' chariots. Gerin strung his bow and stowed it on the right side of his car next to his quiver; on the left went an axe. Like many of the Fox's vassals, Van affected to despise the bow as an unmanly weapon. His seven-foot spear was his favorite arm, and he bore sword, dagger, and a wickedly spiked mace on his belt. Their shields, yard-wide discs of bronze-faced wood and leather, topped the car's low sidewalls when put in their brackets. Gerin's was deliberately dulled, Van's burnished bright. Despite their contrasting styles, the two formed one of the most feared teams on the border.

Gerin's driver, a gangling youth named Raffo, leaped into the chariot. A six-foot shield of heavy leather was slung on a baldric over his left shoulder; it gave Gerin cover from which to shoot. Taking up the reins, Raffo skillfully picked his way through the confusion.

After what seemed far too much time to the Fox, his men gathered in loose formation just behind the gatehouse. Shrieks from beyond the keep told plain as need be that the Trokmoi were plundering his serfs of what little they had. Archers on the palisade kept up a sputtering duel with the barbarians, their targets limited to those the lightning showed.

At Gerin's shouted command, the gatehouse crew flung wide the strong-hinged gates and let the

11

drawbridge thump down. The chariots lumbered into action, trailing mucky wakes. Van's bellowed imprecations cut off in mid-oath when he saw the bridge. "By my beard," he grunted, his guttural accent harsh, "where did it come from?"

"Magicked up, without a doubt," Gerin said, and wished he were as calm as he sounded. No Trokmê hedge-wizard could have called that span into being—nor could the elegant and talented mages of the Sorcerers' Guild in the City of Elabon.

An arrow whining past his ear shattered his brief reveries. Trokmoi swarmed out of the peasant village to meet his men; they had no mind to let their looting be stopped. "Viredorix!" they shouted, and "Balamung!"—a name the Fox did not know. The Elabonians roared back, "Gerin the Fox!" and the two bands met in bloody collision.

A northerner appeared at the left side of the Fox's chariot, sword in hand. The rain plastered his long red hair and flowing mustaches against his head; he wore no helm. The reek of ale was thick about him.

It was easy to read his mind. Van would have to twist his body to use his spear, Raffo had his hands full, and Gerin, who had just shot, could never get off another arrow before the Trokmê's blade pierced him. Feeling like a gambler playing with loaded dice, the Fox snatched up his axe with his left hand and drove it into the barbarian's skull. The Trokmê toppled, a look of outraged surprise still on his face.

Van had caught the action from the corner of his eye. He exploded into laughter. "What a rare

12

sneaky thing it must be to be left-handed," he chuckled.

More barbarians were hustling stolen cattle, pigs, sheep, and serfs across the gleaming bridge to their homeland. The villains had had no chance against the northern wolves; huddled in their huts against the storm and the wandering ghosts of the night, they were easy meat. A few had tried to fight, and their crumpled bodies lay beside their homes. Sickle, flail, and scythe were no match for the sword, spear, shield, helm, and bow of the Trokmê nobles, though their retainers were often little better armed than the peasants. Gerin felt something almost akin to pity as he drove an arrow into one of these and watched him thrash his life away, but knew the northerner would have had no second thoughts about gutting him.

A few Trokmoi had managed to light torches despite the deluge; they smoked and sputtered in the woodsrunners' hands, but the rain made the thatched roofs and wattle walls of the cottages all but impossible to light.

With a wave and a shout Gerin sent half his chariots after the pillagers. His own car was in the middle of the village when he shouted, "Pull up!" Raffo obediently slowed; Gerin slung his quiver over his shoulder, then he and Van slid their shields onto their arms and leaped into the mire. Raffo wheeled the horses and made for the safety of Fox Keep's walls. The chariot-riders not chasing the looters followed the Fox to the ground; panting footmen rushed up to stiffen their line.

A Trokmê sprang on the baron's back before he could find his footing in the slime. His bow flew from his hand. The two struggling men fell together, the barbarian's dagger seeking Gerin's heart but foiled by his cuirass. He jabbed an elbow into the Trokmê's unarmored middle; he grunted and loosened his grasp. Both scrambled for their feet, but Gerin was the quicker. His foot lashed out in a roundhouse kick, and the spiked sole of his sandal ripped away half the Trokmê's face. With a dreadful shriek the marauder sprawled in the ooze, his features a gory mask.

Duin the Bold thundered by on a horse; though his legs were clenched round its barrel, he still wobbled on the beast's bare back. Since a rider did not have both hands free to use a bow and could not deliver any sort of spearthrust without going over his horse's tail, Gerin thought fighting from horseback a foolish notion, but his fierce little vassal clung to the idea with the tenacity of a bear-baiting dog. Duin cut down one startled Trokmê with his sword, but when he slashed at another the northerner ducked under his stroke and gave him a hefty push. He fell in the mud with a splash; the horse fled. The Trokmê was bending over his prostrate victim when an Elabonian with a mace stove in his skull from behind.

Van was in his element. Never happier than when on the field, he was howling a battle song in a language Gerin did not know. His spear drank the blood of one mustachioed barbarian; panther-quick, he brought its bronze-shod butt back to smash the teeth of another raider who had thought to take him from behind. A third Trokmê rushed at him with an axe. The barbarian's wild swipe went wide, as did Van's answering thrust; the im-pulse of the blows left them breast to breast. Van dropped his spear and seized the barbarian's neck

14

with his huge fist. He shook him once, as a dog does a rat, and the crack of parting vertebrae was a dire thing to hear.

The baron did not share his comrade's red joy in slaughter. The main satisfaction he took from killing was the knowledge that the shuddering corpse at his feet was one enemy who would never trouble him again. As far as he could, he stood aloof from the internecine quarrels of his fellow-barons, fighting only when provoked, and fell enough to be provoked but seldom.

Toward the Trokmoi, though, he bore a cold, bitter hatred. At first it had been fueled by the slaying of his father and brother, but now revenge was but a small part of it. The woodsrunners, it seemed, lived only to destroy, and all too often his border holding tasted of that destruction, shielding the softer, more civilized southlands from the sudden bite of arrows and the baying of barbarians in the night.

Almost without thinking, he ducked under a flung stone. Another glanced from his helmet and filled his head with a brief shower of stars. A spear grazed his thigh; an arrow pierced his shield but was turned by his corselet. His archers shot back, filling the air with death. Men in moiling knots cursed, grunted, wrestled, and hewed at each other, and spouting bodies disappeared in the mud to be trampled by friend and foe alike. The Trokmoi swarmed round Gerin's armored troopers like snarling wolves round bears, but little by little they were driven back from the village toward their bridge. Their chieftains still made fierce charges across the Fox's fertile wheatfields, crushing his men beneath the flailing hooves of

15

their woods-ponies, sending yard-long arrows through cuirasses into soft flesh, and lopping off heads and arms with their great slashing swords.

At their fore was Viredorix. He had led his clan for nearly as long as Gerin had been alive, but his splendid red mustachios were unfrosted. Almost as tall as Van, if less wide in the shoulders, he was proud in gilded armor and wheel-crested bronze helm. His chariot was adorned with golden fylfots and the ears of men he had slain. His right hand held a dripping sword, his left the head of an Elabonian who had tried to stand against him.

His long, knobby-cheekboned face split in a grin when he spied Gerin. "It's himself himself," he roared, "come to be corbies' meat like the father of him. Thinking to be a man before your ape of a friend, are you laddie?" His Elabonian was fluent enough, but flavored by his own tongue. Van roared back at him; Gerin, silent, set himself for the charge. Viredorix swung up his sword. His driver, a gaunt, black-robed man the Fox did not know, whipped his beasts forward.

On came the chariot, the hooves of its horses pounding like doom. Gerin was lifting his shield to beat back Viredorix's first mighty stroke when Van's spear flashed over his shoulder and took one of the onrushing ponies full in the chest.

With the awful scream only wounded horses make, the shaggy pony reared and then fell, dragging its harnessmate down with it. The chariot overturned and shattered, sending one wheel flying and spilling both riders into the muck. Gerin ran forward to finish Viredorix, but the Trokmê lit rolling and rushed to meet him. "A fine thing will the skull of you be over my gate," he shouted, and

16

then their blades joined with a clash of sparks and there was no more time for words.

Slashing and chopping, Viredorix surged forward, trying to overwhelm his smaller foe at the first onset. Gerin parried desperately; he would have been sliced in two had any of the Trokmê's cuts landed. When Viredorix's blade bit so deep into the edge of his shield that it stuck for a moment, the Fox seized the chance for a thrust of his own, but Viredorix knocked his questing point aside with a dagger in his left hand; he had lost his bloody trophy when his chariot foundered.

The barbarian would not tire. Gerin's sword was heavy in his hand, his battered shield a lump of lead on his arm, but Viredorix only grew stronger. He was bleeding from a cut under his chin and another on his arm, but his attack never slowed. *Crash! Crash!* An overhand blow smashed the Fox's shield to kindling, the next ripped through his armor and drew a track of fire down his ribs. With a groan, he went to one knee. Thinking him finished, the Trokmê loomed over him, eager to take his head. But Gerin was not yet done. His sword shot up and out with all the force of his body behind it, and its point tore out Viredorix's throat. Dark in the gloom, his lifeblood fountained forth as he fell, both hands clutching futilely at his neck.

The baron dragged himself to his feet. Van came up beside him; there was a fresh cut on his brawny forearm, but his mace dripped blood and brains and his face was wreathed in smiles. He brandished the gory weapon and shouted, "Come on, Captain! We've broken them!"

"Is it to go through me you're thinking?"

17

Gerin's head jerked up. The Trokmê's voice seemed to have come from beside him, but the only northerner within fifty yards was Viredorix's scrawny driver. He wore no armor under his sodden black robes and carried no weapon, but he was striding forward with the confidence of a demigod.

"Stand aside, fool," Gerin said. "I have no stomach for killing an unarmed man."

"Then have not a care in the world, southron darling, for I'll be the death of you and not the other way round at all." Lightning cracked, giving Gerin a glimpse of pale skin stretched drumhead tight over skull and jaw. Like a cat's, the northerner's eyes gave back the light in a green flash. He raised his arms and began to chant. An invocation poured forth, sonorous and guttural, and Gerin's blood froze in his veins as he recognized the magic-steeped speech of the dreaming river valleys of ancient Kizzuwatna. He knew that tongue, and knew it did not belong in the mouth of a swaggering woodsrunner. The Trokmê dropped his hands, screaming, *"Ethrog, O Luhuzantiyas!"*

A horror from the hells of the haunted east appeared before him. Its legs, torso, and head were human, the face even grimly handsome: swarthy, hooknosed, and proud, beard falling in curling ringlets over broad chest. But its arms were the snapping chelae of a monster scorpion, and a scorpion's jointed tail grew from the base of its spine, sting gleaming at the tip. With a bellow that should have come from the throat of a bull, the demon Luhuzantiyas sprang at Gerin and Van.

It was a fight out of a nightmare. Quicker on its feet than any human, the demon used its tail like a living spear. The sting flashed by Gerin's face, so

18

close that he caught the acrid reek of its poison. It scored a glittering line across Van's corselet. Those terrible claws chewed his shield to bits, and only a backward leap saved his arm. The warriors landed blow after blow, but the demon would not go down, though dark ichor pumped from a score of wounds and one claw was sheared away. Not until Van, with a strength born of loathing, smashed skull and face to bloody pulp with frenzied strokes of his mace did it fall. Even then it writhed and thrashed in the mire, still seeking its foes.

Gerin felt his blood trickle warm down his side. He drew in a long, shuddering breath. "Now, wizard," he grated, "join your devil in the fiery pit that spawned it."

The Trokmê had put twenty or so paces between himself and the Fox, but his laugh—an unclean chuckle that scraped across Gerin's nerves—made plain his lack of fear. He bowed mockingly. "It's a strong man you are, lord Gerin the Fox"—the contempt he packed into that stung—"and this day is yours. But we'll meet again; aye, indeed we will. My name, lord Gerin, is Balamung. Mark it well, for you're after hearing it twice the now, and hearing it again you will be."

"Twice?" Gerin did not say it aloud, but Balamung heard.

"Not even remembering, are you? Well, 'twas three years agone I came south, having it in the mind of me to take up sorcery. You had me sleep in the stables, with the reeking horses and all, for some fatgut from the south and his party of pimps filled the keep all to busting, you said. When the next time comes for me to be sleeping at Fox Keep—and 'twill be soon—'twill no be in the

19

stables.

"So south I went, stinking of horsedung, and in the City of Elabon only their hinder parts did the Sorcerers' Collegium show me. The gall of them to be calling me a savage, and that to my face, mind! After you, it's them to be paying their price.

"For, you see, quit I didna. I wandered through desert and mountain, and learned from warlocks and grizzled hermits and squinting scribes who cared not about a 'prentice's accent, if he'd do their bidding. And in a cave lost in the snows of the High Kirs, far above one of the passes the Empire is after having blocked, I found what I had learned to seek, the which is none less than the very Book of Shabeth-Shiri the sorcerer-king of Kizzuwatna long ago. Himself had died there, and when I took the Book from the dead fingers of him it was a puff of smoke he turned to, and blew away. And today it's the Book that's mine, and tomorrow the northlands—and after that, the world is none too big!"

"You lie," Gerin said. "All you will own is a nameless grave, with no-one to comfort your shade."

Balamung laughed again, and now his eyes flamed red with a fire of their own. "Wrong you are, for 'tis the stars themselves tell me no grave will ever hold me. They tell me more, too, for it's the gates of your precious keep they show me all beat to flinders, and that inside two turns of the bloody second moon."

"You lie," Gerin growled again. He ran forward, ignoring the pain lancing up from his wound. Bony hands on hips, Balamung stood watching him. The Fox lifted his blade; Balamung was unmoving, even when it came hissing down to cleave him from crown to breastbone.

The stroke met only empty air; Gerin staggered and almost fell, for, like the light of a candle suddenly snuffed, the wizard was gone. His derisive laugh rang in Gerin's ears for a long moment, then it too faded. "Father Dyaus above!" the shaken Fox exclaimed

Van muttered an oath in an unknown tongue. "Well, Captain," he said, "there's your warlock."

Gerin did not argue it.

The Trokmoi seemed to lose their nerve when the sorcerer disappeared. Faster and faster they streamed over Balamung's bridge, their feet silent on its misty surface. Only a snarling rearguard held Gerin's men at bay. They too slipped away to safety one by one, and with deep-throated roars of triumph the Elabonians swarmed after them.

Like a phantasm compounded of coils of smoke, the bridge vanished into the night as if it had never been. Warriors screamed with terror as they plunged into the foaming Niffet, the bronze weighing about their shoulders dragging them to a watery doom. On the shore men doffed armor with frantic haste and splashed into the water to try to save their comrades. Jeering Trokmoi on the northern bank shot at victims and rescuers alike.

It took two men to save Duin. Impetuous as always, he had been farthest along the bridge when it evaporated, and he could not swim. Somehow he managed to stay afloat until the first rescuer reached him, but so desperate was his grip that both would have drowned had not another swimmer been nearby. A few others were hauled out as

21

well, but Balamung's trap took more than a dozen.

A plashing downstream made Gerin whirl. Matter-of-fact as any river godlet, Drago the Bear came out of the water, wringing his long beard like a peasant wench with her man's breeches. Incredibly, armor still gleamed on his breast.

If anyone could survive such a dip, thought Gerin, it would be Drago. He was strong as an ox and lacked the imagination to be frightened by anything. Still, his retainers were devoted to him and, if he was not brilliant, the Fox found it hard to imagine him disloyal.

"Nasty," he rumbled in a voice like falling trees. He might have been talking about the weather.

"Aye," muttered an abstracted Gerin. At the same moment the bridge melted away, the rain had stopped. Pale, dim Nothos, nearing full, gleamed in a suddenly star-flecked sky, while ruddy Elleb, now waning toward third quarter, was just beginning to wester. The other two moons, golden Math and quick-moving Tiwaz, were both near new and hence invisible.

Hustling along a double handful of disheveled prisoners, most of them wounded, the weary army made its way back to the keep. A large contingent of Gerin's serfs met them at the village. They capered about making fools of themselves, screaming their thanks for having their crops saved in a dialect so rustic that even Gerin, who had heard it from birth, found it hard to understand.

Gerin ordered ten oxen slaughtered, laying the fat-wrapped thigh-bones on the altars of Dyaus and the war-god Deinos, which stood in his great

22

hall. The rest of the meat vanished into his men. To wash it down, barrel after barrel of smooth, foaming ale and sweet mead were broached and emptied. The makings of a full-scale celebration took shape. Men who found combat raising other urges pursued serving wenches and peasant girls, many of whom made only token efforts at evasion.

At first the baron did not join the merrymaking himself. He tended to his wound (luckily not deep), applying an ointment of honey, lard, and astringent herbs; he winced at their bite. Then he had the brightest-looking captive, a tall mournful blond barbarian who kept his left hand clutched to a torn right shoulder, bandaged and brought into a storeroom. While two troopers stood by with drawn swords, Gerin cleaned his nails with a dagger from his belt. He said nothing.

The silence bothered the Trokmê, who fidgeted nervously. "What is it you'd want of me?" he burst out at last. "It's Cliath son of Ailech I am, of a house noble for more generations than I have toes and fingers, and no right at all do you have to treat me like some low footpad."

"What right have you," Gerin asked mildly, "to rob and burn my land and kill my men? I could flay the hide off your carcass in inch-wide strips and give it to my dogs to eat while what was left of you watched, and there would be no-one to say I did not have the right. Thank your gods Wolfar did not catch you; he would do it. But tell me what I need to know, and I will set you free. Otherwise," his eyes flicked to the two hard men by him, "I'll walk out this door, and ask no questions after."

One of Cliath's eyes was swollen shut; the other

23

glowed green in the dim lamplight. "What would be keeping you from doing that anyway, once I've talked?"

Gerin shrugged. "It's almost eight years I've held this keep. Men on both sides of the Niffet know what my word is worth. And on this you have that word: you'll have no second chance."

Cliath studied him. The Trokmê made a move as if to rub his chin, but grimaced and thought better of it. He sighed. "What would you know of me, then?"

"Tell me this: what do you know of the black-robed warlock who calls himself Balamung?"

"Och, that kern? Till this raid it's little I've had to do with him, and wanted less. It's bad cess to any honest man to have truck with a wizard, say I, for all he brings loot. No glory in beating en-sorcelled foes is there, no more than in cutting the throat of a pig, and him tied, too. But those who go with him grow fat, and the few as stand against him, and in ways so pretty as having the skins of them flayed off. I mind me of one fellow—poor wight!—who no slower than a sneeze was nought more than a pile of white twisty, slimy worms— and the stench of him! Nigh on a year and a half is it since the omadhaun came to us, and for all we're friends now with Bricriu's clan and thieving Meriasek's, still I long for the days when a man could take a head without asking the leave of a dried-up little turd like Balamung. Him and his dog-futtering talisman!" the Trokmê spat on the hard-packed dirt floor.

"Talisman?"

"Aye. With my own eyes I've seen it. 'Tis squarish, perhaps as long as my forearm, and so wide, but not near so thick, you understand, and opening out to double that. And when he'd fain

24

bewitch someone or magic up something, why the talisman lights up almost like a torch. With my own eyes I've seen it," Claith repeated.

"Can you read?" Gerin asked.

"No, nor write, no more than I can fly. Why in the name of the gods would you care to know that?"

"Never mind," Gerin said. "I know enough now." More than I want, he added to himself; Bricriu's clan and Meriasek's had been at feud since the days of their grandfathers. He tossed the knife to the barbarian, who tucked it into the top of one of his high rawhide boots. The Fox led him through the main hall, ignoring the stares his vassals gave him. He told his startled gatekeepers to let out Cliath, and said to him, "How you cross the river is your affair, but with that blade I hope you won't be waylaid by my serfs."

Good eye shining, Cliath held out his left hand. "A poor clasp, but I'm proud to make it. Och, what a clansmate you'd have been."

Gerin took the offered hand but shook his head. "No," he said, "I'd sooner live on my own land than take away my neighbor's. Now go, before I remember the trouble I'm giving myself by turning you loose." As the northerner trotted down the hill Gerin was already on his way back to the rollicking great hall, a frown on his face. Truly Deinos had loosed his terrible hounds in the northern forests, and the baron was the game they sought.

After he had downed five or six tankards, though, things looked rosier. He staggered up the stairs to his room, arm round the waist of one of his serving wenches. But even as he cupped her soft

25

breasts later, part of his mind saw Castle Fox a smoking ruin, and fire and death all along the border.

chapter 2

It was past noon when he awoke. From the noises coming from below, the roistering had never ceased. Probably no-one was on the walls, either, he thought disgustedly; could Balamung have roused his men to a second attack, he would have had Fox Keep in the palm of his fleshless hand.

The girl was already gone; he dressed and went down to the great hall, looking for half a dozen of his leading liegemen. There he found Van and Rollan the Aurochs-slayer still rehashing the battle, drawing lines on the table in sticky mead. Fandor the Fat had a beaker of mead, too, but he was drinking from it. That was his usual sport, and his red nose and awesome capacity testified to it. Drago was asleep on the floor, his body swathed in furs; beside him snored Simrin Widin's son. Duin was nowhere to be found.

The Fox woke Simrin and Drago and bullied his lieutenants up the stairs to his library. Grumbling, they found seats round the central table and stared suspiciously at the shelves full of neatly-pigeon-hold scrolls and codices bound in leather and gold leaf. Most of them were as illiterate as Cliath and held reading an affectation, but Gerin was a good enough man of his hands to let them overlook his eccentricity. Still, the books and the quiet overawed them a bit, and today he needed that.

He scratched his bearded chin and remembered how horrified they'd been when after his father had been killed, he'd come back from the southlands clean-shaven. Duin's father, dour old Borbeto the Grim, had been managing the barony until his return, and when he saw Gerin he had roared, "Is Duren's son a fancy-boy?" Gerin only grinned and answered, "Ask your daughter," and the shouts of laughter won the barons to him.

Duin wandered in, still fumbling at his breeches. Bawdy chuckles greeted him. Fandor called, "Easier to stay on a lass than a horse, is it?"

"It is, and more fun besides," Duin grinned, plainly none the worse for his dunking. He turned to Gerin, sketched a salute. "What's on your mind, lord?"

"Among other things," Gerin said drily, "the bridge that was almost your end."

"Downright uncanny, I call it," murmured Rollan. He spoke thickly, for his slashed lip had three stitches holding it shut. Tall, solid, and dark, he ran his fief with some skill, fought bravely, and never let a new thought trouble his mind.

"Me, I have no truck with wizards," Drago said righteously. He sneezed. "Damn! I've taken cold!" He went on, "There's no way to trust a body like that. Noses always in a scroll, think they're better than simple folk."

"Remember where you are, fool," Simrin

28

Widin's son hissed.

"No offense meant, of course, lord," Drago said hastily.

"Of course," Gerin sighed. "Now let me tell you what I learned last night." The faces of his men grew grave as the tale unfolded, and there was a silence when he was through.

Duin broke it. Along with his auburn hair, his fiery temper told of Trokmê blood. Now he thumped a fist down on the table and shouted, "A pox on wizardry! There's but one thing to do about it. We have to hit the whoreson before he can hit us again, and this time with all the northmen, not just Viredorix's clan."

A mutter of agreement ran down the table, but Gerin shook his head. This was what he had to head off at all costs. "There's nothing I'd like better," he lied, "but it won't do. Their mage would squash us like so many bugs on his home ground. But from what the braggart said, we do have some time. What I'd fain do is go south to the City and hire a warlock from the Sorcerers' Collegium there so we can fight magic with magic. I don't relish leaving Fox Keep under the axe, but the task is mine, for I have connections yet in the southlands. We can settle Balamung properly once I'm back."

"It strikes me as a fool's errand, lord," Duin said, plain-spoken as always. "What we need is a good, hard stroke now—"

"Duin, if you want to beard that wizard without one at your back, then you're the fool. If you had to take a keep with a stone-thrower over its gate, you'd find a stone-thrower of your own, wouldn't you?"

"I suppose so," Duin said. His tone was surly,

29

but there were nods round the table. Gerin was relieved; he was coming to the tricky part, and with a little luck he could slip it by them before they noticed.

"Stout fellow!" he said, and went on easily, "Van will need your help here while I'm gone. With him in charge nothing can go too badly wrong."

It didn't work. Even Fandor and Simrin, both of whom had kept their noses buried in their drinking-jacks until now, jerked up their heads. Diffidently, Rollan began, "Begging your pardon, my lord," and Gerin braced for insubordination. It was fast enough coming: "The gods know Van of the Strong Arm has proved himself a man, time and again, and a loyal and true vassal as well. But for all that, he is an outlander and owns no land hereabouts, living with you as he does. It'd be downright unseemly for us, whose families have held our fiefs for generations, to take orders from him."

Gerin gathered himself for an explosion, but before he loosed it he saw his barons nodding their agreement. He caught Van's eye; the outlander shrugged the tiniest of shrugs inside his armor. "If that's how you would have it, so be it," he said. "Van, would it please you to ride with me, then?"

"It would that, Captain," Van said, coming as close as he ever did to Gerin's proper feudal title. "I've never been south of the Kirs, and I've heard enough about the City to make me want to see it."

"Fine," Gerin said. "Duin, you have the highest standing of any here. Do you think you can keep things afloat while I'm away?"

"Aye, or die trying."

30

Gerin feared the latter, but merely said, "Good!" and whispered a prayer under his breath. Duin was more than doughty enough and not stupid, but he lacked common sense.

Drago and Rollan decided to stay at Fox Keep themselves and to leave the defense of their own castles to the vassal contingents they would send home; Gerin dared hope they might be a restraining influence on Duin. After his other liegemen had gone, he spent a couple of hours giving Duin instructions on matters probable, matters possible, and as many matters impossible as his fertile mind could envision. He finished, "For Dyaus' sake, send word along the West March Road and the Emperor's Highway. The border barons must know of this so they can ready themselves for the storm."

"Even Wolfar?"

"As his holding borders mine, news would have to go through him anyway. But it happens the slug is out a-courting, and his man Schild, though he has no love for me, won't kill a messenger for the sport of it. Also, you could do worse than to get Siglorel here; he has the most power of any wizard north of the Kirs, even if he is overfond of his ale. When I last heard he was at the keep of Hovan son of Hagop east of here, trying to cure Hovan's piles."

Duin nodded, hopefully in wisdom. He surprised Gerin by offering a suggestion of his own. "If you're bound to go through with this wizard scheme, lord," he said, "why not go to Ikos and ask the Sibyl for her advice?"

"You know, that's not a bad thought," Gerin nodded. "I've been that way once before, and it will only cost me an extra day or so."

Next day he decided—not for the first time—that mixing ale and mead was a poor idea. The crisp cool air of early morning settled in his lungs like sludge. His side was stiff and sore, his head ached, and the creaks and groans of the light wagon and steady pound of hooves on stone roadbed, sounds he usually failed to notice, rang loud in his ears. The sun seemed to have singled him out for all its rays.

Worst of all, Van, sure hands tending the reins, was awake and in full song. Holding his throbbing head, Gerin asked, "Don't you know any quiet tunes?"

"Aye, several of them," Van answered, and returned to his interrupted ditty.

Gerin contemplated death and other delights.

At last the song came to an end. "I thank you," Gerin said.

"Nothing at all Captain." Van frowned, then went on, "I think yesterday I was too hellishly worn out to pay as much attention to what you were saying as I should. Why is it such a fell thing for Balamung to have gotten his bony fingers on Shabeth-Shiri's book?"

The Fox was glad to talk, if only to dull the edge of his own worry. "Shabeth-Shiri was the greatest sorcerer-prince of Kizzuwatna long ago: the land where all wizardry began, and where it flourishes to this day. They say he was the first to uncover the laws behind their magic, and set them down in writing to teach his pupils."

"Now, that can't be the book Balamung was boasting of, can it?"

"No; I have a copy of it myself, as a matter of fact. So does everyone who's ever dabbled in magic. It's not a book of spells, but of the principles by which they're cast. But, using those principles, Shabeth-Shiri worked more powerful warlockery than any this poor shuddering world has seen since. Remember, he was prince and mage both, and he fought so many wars he ran short of men, or so the story goes. So he kept his rule alive by raising demons to fight for him, and by many other such cantrips. Think how embarrassed an army that thought itself safe behind a stream would be to have it flood and drown their camp, or turn to blood, or to see fiends charging over a bridge like the one Balamung used against us."

"Embarrassed is scarcely the word, Captain."

"I suppose not. Shabeth-Shiri wrote down all his most mightful spells, too, but in a book he showed to no-one. He meant it for his son, they say, but for all his wizardry he was beaten at last: all the other mages and marshals of Kizzuwatna combined against him, lest he rule the whole world. His son was killed in the sack of his last citadel, Shaushka—"

"Shaushka the Damned? Was that his? I've seen it with my own eyes. It lies in the far north of Kizzuwatna, at the edge of the plains of Shanda, and the plainsmen showed it to me from far away: stark, dark, and dead. Nothing grows there to this day, even after—how many years?"

Gerin shuddered. "Two thousand, if a day. But the conquerors never found Shabeth-Shiri's body, or his book either, though sorcerers have searched for it from that day to this. The legends say some of its pages are of human skin, and it glows with a

33

light of its own when its master uses it.'' The baron gloomily shook his head. ''Cliath saw it, sure as sure.''

''A nice fellow, this Shabeth-Shiri, and I think he'd be proud of the one who has his Book now. It seems all Kizzuwatnans have a taste for blood, though,'' Van said. ''Once when I was traveling with the nomads—'' Gerin never found out about the Kizzuwatnan Van had fallen foul of, for at that moment two hurtling bodies burst from the oaks that grew almost to within bowshot of the road.

One was a stag, proud head now low as it fled in desperate terror from its pursuer. But it had not taken more than three bounds when a tawny avalanche struck it from behind and smashed it to the grass. Great stabbing fangs tore into its throat, once, twice. Blood spurted and slowed; its hooves drummed and then were still.

Crouched over its kill, the longtooth snarled a warning at the travelers. It settled its short hind legs under its belly and began to feed. Its little stumpy tail quivered in absurd delight as it tore steaming hunks of flesh from the carcass of the stag. When the men stopped to watch, it growled deep in its throat and dragged its prey into the cover of the woods.

Van was all for flushing it out again, but Gerin demurred; like rogue aurochs, longtooths were best hunted by parties larger than two. Rather grumpily, Van put away his spear. ''Sometimes, Gerin,'' he complained, ''you take all the fun out of life.''

The Fox did not answer; his head still hurt. But his gloomy mood slowly cleared as the sun rose higher in the sky. He looked about with more than a little pride, for the lands he ruled were rich ones.

And, he thought, the wealth they made stayed on them.

Traffic on the great road was light so near the border. The only traveler Gerin and Van met the first day was a wandering merchant. A thin doleful man, he nodded gravely as he headed north, leading a train of laden donkeys. From his left shoulder his companion, a calico cat with mismatched eyes and only one ear, glared at Gerin as they passed.

As night began to near, the baron bought a brace of fowls from a farmer who dwelt by the road. Van shook his head as he watched his friend haggle with the peasant. "Why not just take what you need, like any lord?" he asked. "The kern is your subject, after all."

"True enough, but he's not my slave. A baron who treats his serfs like beasts of burden will see his castle come down round his ears the first time his crops fail. Serve him right, too, the fool."

When they stopped for the evening, Gerin wrung the neck of one hen and drained its blood into a trough he dug in the rich black soil. "That should satisfy any roving spirits," he said, quickly plucking the bird and skewering it on a spit to roast over his campfire.

"Any that wouldn't sooner drink *our* blood instead," Van half-agreed. "Captain, out on the plains of Shanda the ghosts have real fangs, and they aren't shy of watchfires. Only the charms the nomads' shamans magic up can keep them at bay—and sometimes not those, either, if most of the moons are dark. A bad place."

Gerin believed him; any land his hard-bitten comrade was chary of was a good place to avoid.

35

They drew straws for the first watch. Within seconds Van was curled in his bedroll, snoring like a thunderstorm. Gerin watched Tiwaz and Math, both thin crescents almost lost in the skirts of twilight, follow the sun down to the horizon. As they sank, full Nothos rose, and under his weak grayish light field and forest alike were half-seen mysteries. Small night-creatures chirped and hummed. Gerin let the fire die into embers, and the ghosts came.

As always, the eye refused to admit their shape, slipping away before it could be grasped. They swarmed round the pool of blood like great carrion flies, and their buzzing filled Gerin's mind. Some shouted in tongues so ancient their very names were lost, while others could almost be understood, but there was no sound to be heard, only clamor and loss and wailing. The Fox knew that if he tried to gasp one of the flittering shapes it would slip through his fingers like so much mist, for the dead kept at best but a pallid semblance of life. Grateful for the boon of blood, they tried to give him such redes as they thought wise, but only a noise like that of rushing winds filled his head. He knew if he had not granted them the gift, or if the fire had not been there, they would likey have driven him mad.

He kept watch until midnight, staring at stars and full Nothos and the half-seen shapes of spirits until Elleb, a copper disc almost half chewed away, was well clear of the dark woods on the horizon. No man disturbed him: few were the travelers so bold as to risk moving in the dark of the sun.

When Gerin roused him, Van woke with the in-

36

stant awareness of a seasoned warrior. "The ghosts are bad tonight," the baron mumbled, and then he was asleep.

Van announced the dawn with a whoop that hauled the Fox from the depths of sleep. Trying to pry his eyes open, he said, "I feel like my head is filled with sand. 'Early in the morning' says the same thing twice."

"An hour before noon is counted as morning, is it not?"

"Aye, it is, and too bloody early in the bargain. Oh for the days when I was in the City and not one of the wise men I listened to thought of opening his mouth before noon."

Gerin gnawed leathery journeybread, dried fruit, and smoked sausage, washing them down with bitter beer. He almost gagged on the bread; the stuff had the virtue of keeping nearly forever, and he understood why, for the bugs liked it no better than he. He sighed, stretched, and climbed into his armor, wincing as his helm slipped down over one ear bent permanently outward by a northerner's club in some long-forgotten skirmish. "The birds are shining, the sun is chirping, and who am I to complain?" he said.

Van gave him a curious glance. "You feeling all right, Captain?" he asked, a note of real concern in his voice.

"Yes and no," Gerin said thoughtfully. "But for the first time since I came back from the city, it doesn't matter at all. Things are out of my hands for a while now, and if someone pisses in the soup-pot, why, Duin will just have to try and take care of it without me. It's a funny feeling, you know. I'm half glad to be free and half afraid things will

37

fall apart without me. It's like running a long way and then stopping short: you've got used to the strain, and feel wrong without it."

They moved south steadily, but not in silence. Van extracted a clay flute from his kit and made the morning hideous with it. Gerin politely asked him if he had been taking music lessons from the ghosts, but he shrugged a massive shrug and kept on tweedling.

A pair of guardhouses flanked the road where it crossed from Gerin's lands to those of Palin the Eagle. Two sets of troopers sprawled in the roadway, dicing the day away. At the creak of the egon they abandoned their game and looked to their weapons.

Gerin looked down his long nose at the wary archers. "Hail!" he said. "Would that you had been so watchful last summer, when you let Wacho and his brigands sneak south without so much as a challenge."

The guard captain shuffled his feet. "Lord, how was I to know he'd forged his safe-conduct?"

"By the hand of it, and the spelling," Gerin retorted. "The lout could barely write. It matters little now, but if it happens again you'll find a new lord, probably in the underworld. Do we pass your inspection?"

"You do that, lord," the guard said, and waved the wagon on. Gerin drew sword as he passed the ancient boundary stone separating his holdings from Palin's, and Palin's guardsmen returned his salute. For long generations the two houses had been at peace, and the stone, its time-worn runes now covered by gray-green moss, had sunk almost half its height into the soft earth.

Once past the guards, Van turned and said to Gerin, "You know, Fox, when I first came to your land I thought Palin the Eagle must be some fine warrior, to judge from what his folk called him. How was I to know they were talking of his nose?"

"He's no Carlun come again, I will allow that," Gerin chuckled. "But he and his vassals do keep order well enough that I don't fear a night or so in the open in his lands, or perhaps with one of his lordlets."

"You don't want himself to guest you?"

"No indeed. In his keep there's an unmarried sister who must be rising forty by now, and desperate, poor lass. She cooks for him too, and badly. The last time I ate with Palin I thought the belly-sickness had me, and not just a sour stomach."

When the travelers did stop for the night it was at the ramshackle keep of one of Palin's vassals, Raff the Ready. A blocky boulder of a man, he was very much of the old school, wearing a forked beard that almost reached his waist. His unflappable solidity reminded the Fox of Drago; less hearteningly, so did his total disdain for cleanliness. Withal, he set a fine table. He had killed a cow that day, and along with the beef there was a stew of frogs and mussels from a nearby pond, fresh-baked bread, blueberries and blueberry tarts, and a fine, nutlike ale with which to wash them down.

Gerin sighed in contentment, loosened his belt, belched, and then, reluctantly, gave Raff his news. His host looked uneasy and promised to spread the word. "You think your men won't be able to hold them at the Niffet, then?" he asked.

39

"I'm very much afraid they won't."

"Well, I'll tell my neighbors, not that it'll do much good. All of us are looking south, not north, waiting for the trouble in Bevon's barony to spill over into ours."

"There's fighting there?" Van asked hopefully.

"Aye, there is that. All four of Bevon's sons are brawling over the succession, and him not even dead yet. One of them ran twenty sheep off Palin's land, too, the son of a whore."

With that warning they left early, almost before dawn. They carried a torch to keep the ghosts at bay, but even so Gerin's skin crawled with dread until the spirits fled the rays of the sun.

He spent a nervous morning hurrying south through Bevon's strife-torn barony. Every one of Bevon's vassals kept his castle shut tight. The men on the walls gave Gerin and Van hard stares, but no-one made a move to stop them.

Around noon they heard fighting down an approaching side-road. Van looked interested, but Gerin was far more intent on reaching the City than getting drawn into an imbroglio not his own. The choice was quickly taken out of his hands. Two spearmen and an archer, plainly fleeing, burst onto the highway. The archer took one hasty glance at Gerin and Van, shouted, "More traitors!" and let fly at the travelers at point-blank range. His shaft sailed between them, perhaps because he could not pick one as target.

He got no second shot. Gerin had been sitting with bow ready to hand, and no confusion spoiled his aim. But even as the archer fell, an arrow through his throat, his comrades charged the wagon.

The fight was savage but short, for the foot-soldiers seemed already to have despaired of their lives, thinking only of killing before they fell. Cool as usual in a fight, the Fox soon found opportunity to duck under his foe's guard and slide the point of his blade between the luckless fellow's ribs. The man coughed blood and died. Gerin turned to help Van, but his friend needed no aid. A stroke of his axe had shattered his man's spearshaft, another had cloven through helm and skull alike. Only a tiny cut above his knee showed he had fought at all. He rubbed at it, grumbling, "The bastard pinked me. I must be getting old."

The triumph left only the taste of ashes in Gerin's mouth. What fools the men of Elabon were, to be fighting among themselves while a storm to sweep them all away was growing in the northern forests! And now he was as guilty as any. Three warriors who might have been bold against the Trokmoi were stiffening corpses in the road-way because of him. That his mission justified the slayings was scant consolation, for in his heart he had little faith in the ability of the southern wizards to withstand Balamung's goetic potency.

The Fox sighed with relief when at last he spied the guard-house of Bevon's southern neighbor, Ricolf the Red. He was not surprised to see it had a double complement of men.

The baron returned the courteous greetings Ricolf's guardsmen gave him. He knew a few of them, for he had spent several pleasant weeks at Ricolf's keep on his last journey to the southlands. "It's been too long, lord Gerin," said one of the guards. "Ricolf will be glad to see you."

"And I him; he was like a second father to me."

41

"Peace be with you, wayfarers," Ricolf's man called as they drove past.

"And to you also peace." Van made the proper response, for he held the reins. He had been quick to pick up the customs of Gerin's land.

The sun was dying in the west and Gerin felt the first low keening of long-dead wraiths when Ricolf's castle came into view, crowned by a scarlet banner. Somewhere high overhead an eagle screamed. Van's keen eyes searched the sky until he found the moving speck. "On our right," he said. "There's a good omen, if you like."

"I mislike taking omens from birds," Gerin said. "They're too public. Who's to say a foretelling is meant for him and not some lout in the next holding who has to squint to see it?"

A boy's clear voice floated from Ricolf's watchtower: "Who comes to the holding of Ricolf the Red?"

"I am Gerin, called the Fox, guest-friend to your master Ricolf, and with me is my friend and companion, Van of the Strong Arm. By Dyaus and Rilyn, god of friendship, we claim shelter for the night."

"Bide a moment." There was a pause, and then Gerin heard Ricolf's deep voice exclaim, "What? Let them in, fool, let them in!" The drawbridge swung down and the lad cried, "In the names of Dyaus and Rilyn, welcome, guest-friend Gerin! Be you welcome also Van of the Strong Arm."

Ricolf's keep, more sophisticated than Gerin's frontier fortress, had stone outwalls instead of a log palisade. Its moat was broad and deep; the slick surface of the water was splashed with clusters of limp-looking plants. A vile stench rose from the moat, and sinuous ripples made Gerin suspect water plants were not the only things to call it home.

Ricolf greeted his guests at the gatehouse. He was stout, perhaps fifty, with a square, ruddy face and blue eyes. His tunic and trousers were brightly checked and modish in cut, but the sword swinging at his belt was a plain, well-battered weapon that had seen much use. There was more gray in his red hair and beard than Gerin remembered, and lines of worry the Fox had never seen before bracketed his eyes and mouth.

When Gerin scrambled down from the wagon, Ricolf enfolded him in a bearhug, pumping his hand and thumping his back. "Great Dyaus above, lad, is it ten years? They've made a man of you! Ten years indeed, and we not living five days' ride from each other. This must never happen again!"

Untangling himself, Gerin said, "True enough, but I doubt if either of us had had a five-day stretch free and clear in all those years." He explained why he was traveling south; Ricolf nodded in grim comprehension. Gerin went on, "If what traders say is true, you've had your own troubles."

"I did, until I sent my unloving cousin Sarus to the afterworld this past winter," Ricolf agreed. He focused on Van. "Is this your new lieutenant? I thought what news of him I heard so much nonsense, but I see it was just the truth."

"My comrade, rather," Gerin said, and made the introduction. Van acknowledged it with grave respect. His broad hand, back thick-thatched with golden hair, swallowed Ricolf's in its clasp.

"I greet you as well, Van of the Strong Arm.

43

Use my home as your own for so long as you would," Ricolf said. "Speaking of which," he turned back to Gerin, "would you like to scrub off the dust of the road in my bath-house before we eat? You have the time, I think."

"Bath-house?" Gerin's ears sprang to attention. "I thought I'd have to freeze my crotch in the streams or reek like a dungheap until I got south of the mountains."

Ricolf looked pleased. "So far as I know, I have the first. I had it put in last summer, when I first sent messages to the unmarried barons of the north-country—and to some south of the Kirs, too—that any who thought himself worthy of my daughter Elise's hand should come here, so I could decide which man I thought most suited to her. My wife Yrse gave me no sons who lived, you know, nor have I hopes for any legitimate ones now, as I've no real intention of marrying again now that she's gone. I had three bastard boys, and one a lad of promise, too, but the chest-fever carried them off two winters back, poor lads, so when I die the holding passes to Elise and whoever she weds. Gerin, you must have got my invitation to join us; I know you're still unwed."

"I did, but I had an arrow through my shoulder. It was a nasty one, and I was afraid the hole would rot if I traveled too soon. I sent my regrets."

"Aye, that's right, so you did. I remember now. I was truly sorry; you've done yourself a fine job since Duren and Dagref, er, died."

"It wasn't the trade I was trained for," Gerin shrugged. "My father always counted on Dagref; besides being older than me, he was a fighter born. Who would have thought the Trokmoi could get

44

the two of them at once? I know my father never did. As for me, I'm still alive, so I suppose I haven't disgraced myself.''

He changed the subject; remembering his father still hurt. ''Now you'd better show me where that bath-house of yours is before your dogs decide I'm part of the midden.'' He scratched the ears of a shaggy, reddish hound sniffing his ankles. Its tail switched back and forth as it grinned up at him, tongue lolling out. A half-memory flickered; he pursued it but could not make it light.

''Go away, Ruffian!'' Ricolf snapped. The dog ignored him. ''Beast thinks the place belongs to him,'' Ricolf grumbled. He took Gerin's arm and pointed. ''Right over there, and I'll see to it your horses are tended.''

Ricolf's tubs were carved limestone; the delicate frieze of river godlets and nymphs carved round them told Gerin they'd been hauled up from the south, for local gravers were not so skilled. Soaking in his steaming tub, the Fox said, ''Ricolf gives his suitors nothing but the finest. I never thought I'd feel clean again.''

Van's bulk almost oozed out of his tub, but he grunted contented agreement. He asked, ''What is this daughter of Ricolf's like?''

Gerin paused to rinse suds from his beard. ''Your guess is as good as mine. As near as I can remember, ten years back she was small and skinny, and rather wished she were a boy.''

They dried on furs. Van spent a few minutes polishing imaginary dull places on his cuirass and combing the scarlet crest of his helm. Gerin did not re-don his own armor, choosing instead a sky-blue tunic and black breeches. ''With your gear,'' the

45

baron said, "you could go anywhere, but I'd look a mere private soldier in mine. Even this is none too good; the southerners will doubtless have their hair all curled and oiled and wear these toga things they affect." He waved a limp-wristed hand. "And they talk so pretty, too."

"Don't have much use for them, eh, Captain?"

Gerin smiled wryly. "That's the funniest part of it; I spent the happiest part of my life south of the Kirs. I'm a southerner at heart some ways, I suppose, but I can't let it show at Fox Keep."

Ricolf met them and led them into his long hall. At the west end a great pile of fat-wrapped bones smoked before Dyaus' altar. "You feed the god well," Gerin said.

"He has earned it." Ricolf turned to the men already at the tables. "May I present the baron Gerin, called the Fox, and his companion Van of the Strong Arm. Gentlemen, we have here Rihwin the Fox—"

Gerin stared at the man who shared his title. Rihwin stared back, his clean-shaven face a mask. That alone would have said he was from the south, but he wore a flowing green toga and a golden hoop in his left ear. Gerin liked most southern ways, but he had always thought that a bit excessive.

Ricolf was still talking. "Also Rumold of the Long Bow, Laidrad the Besieger, Wolfar of the Axe—"

Gerin muttered a polite unpleasantry. Wolfar, a dark-skinned lump of a man with bushy eyebrows, coarse black hair, and an unkempt thicket of beard that almost reached his swordbelt, was his western neighbor. They'd fought a bloody skirmish over nothing in particular two winters ago, before

46

Wolfar went to seek Ricolf's daughter.

While Ricolf droned on, introducing more suitors and men of his household, Gerin grew hungrier and hungrier. Finally Ricolf said, "And last but surely not least, my daughter Elise."

The baron was dimly aware of Van sweeping off his helmet and somehow bowing from the waist in full armor. Elise's long golden gown acutely reminded him how much little girls could grow in ten years. He was vaguely regretful she did not follow the bare-bodiced southern style, but it was scarcely necessary. Long brown hair flowed over her creamy shoulders. Her laughing green eyes held him. "I remember you well, Lord Gerin," she said lightly. "When last you were here you bounced me on your knee. Times change, though."

"So they do, my lady," Gerin agreed mournfully.

He took his seat without much attention to his benchmates, and found himself between Rihwin and Wolfar. "Bounced her on your knee, forsooth?" Rihwin said, soft voice turning words in elaborate southern patterns. "I should be less than a truthteller were I to say some such idea had not crossed my mind at one time or another, and perhaps the minds of others here as well. And here we have a man who has accomplished the fondest dreams of a double hand of nobles and more: in good sooth, a fellow manifestly to be watched with the greatest of care." He raised his mug in mocking salute, but Gerin thought the smile on his handsome face was real. The baron drained his own tankard in return. Rihwin seemed to wince as he downed his ale; no doubt he preferred wine.

47

Most southerners did, but north of the Kirs grapes did not grow well.

Gerin felt an elbow nudge his ribs. Wolfar grinned at him, displaying snaggled teeth. Gerin suspected he had were-blood in him; his hairiness varied marvelously as the moons whirled through the sky, and three years before, when Nothos and Math were full at the same time, there had been a tale that he had gone all alone into the forests of the Trokmoi and with his teeth ripped out the throat of any man he met. "How fare you, Fox?" he grunted.

"Well enough until now," Gerin answered smoothly. From the corner of his eye he saw Rihwin cock an eyebrow in an expression he was more used to feeling on his own face than seeing on another. He felt he had passed an obscure test.

His empty belly was growling audibly when the repast made its appearance. Ricolf's cooks did not have the spices and condiments the Fox had known south of the mountains, but the food was good and they did no violence to it. There was beef broth roasted and boiled, fowls fried crisp and brown, mutton, ribs of pork cooked in a tangy sauce, creamy cheese with a firm, tasty outer skin, thick soup from the stockpot, and mountains of fresh-baked bread. Ricolf's good beer was an added delight. Serving wenches ran here and there, food-laden bronze platters in their hands, trying to keep ahead of the gobbling suitors.

Rihwin and one or two others discreetly patted the girls as they went by. Gerin understood their caution; it would not have done for a noble intent on marrying Ricolf's daughter to get one of his wenches with child. Van had no such compunctions. When a well-made lass came by, he kissed her loudly and squeezed her haunch. She squealed and almost dropped her tray. Her face was red as she pulled away, but she was smiling back at him.

The feasters tossed gnawed bones onto the hall's dirt floor, where Ricolf's dogs fought and snarled over them. Whenever the battles grew too noisy a couple of cleaned-up serfs in stout boots toed the hounds apart. Even so, the din was overpowering. So was the smell; the odors of dog and man vied with the smell of cooking meat, and the acrid smoke from the torches and the great hearth next to Dyaus' altar hung in a choking cloud, with only a little going up the flue.

Gerin ate until he could barely move, then settled back, replete and happy. Everyone rose as Elise made her exit, flanked by two maids. When she was gone the serious drinking and gambling began.

Wolfar, as Gerin knew well, was a fanatic for dicing, but tonight, for some reason, he declined to enter the game. "I never bet in my life," he declared loftily, pretending not to hear the Fox's snort.

"I wish I could say that," mourned a loser as his bet was scooped up.

"Why can't you? Wolfar just did," Rihwin said. Gerin grinned at him with genuine liking. In the southlands the smooth insult was a fine art, one the baron had enjoyed but one decidedly too subtle for Castle Fox. Rihwin nodded back; it seemed he had aimed the remark for Gerin's ears. It always warmed the Fox when a southerner born and bred took him for equal; they were a snobbish lot on the other side of the Kirs. That Wolfar was

49

Rihwin's target made things only more delightful.

Rihwin had a capacity for ale that belied his soft looks. Gerin valiantly tried to keep up, emptying his mug again and again until the room spun as he rose. His last clear memory was of Van howling out a nomad battlesong and accompanying himself with the flat of his blade on the tabletop.

To his everlasting amazement, the baron woke up the next morning in a bed, though he had scant notion of how or when he'd reached it. Little wails of delight and Van's hoarsechuckle from the next room told him the outlander had not wasted his night sleeping.

The Fox found a bucket of cold water outside his door and poured it over his head. Spluttering, he wandered down the passageway and into the yard. He found Ricolf halfheartedly practicing with the bow. Though the older man had not tried to pace his guests, he looked wan.

"Is this sort of thing a nightly happening?" Gerin asked.

"The gods forbid! Were it so, I'd have been long dead. No, I plan to announce my decision tonight, and it would be less than natural if the tension didn't build. For near a year I've seen these men—all but Sigiber the Strong, poor wight, who got a spear through his middle—in battle, heard them talk, watched them. Aye, my mind's made up at last."

"Who?"

"Can you keep it quiet? No, that's a foolish question; you could before, pup though you were, and it's not the sort of thing to change in a man. For all his affected ways—I know there are some who call him 'Fop' and not 'Fox'—Rihwin is easi-

50

ly the best of them. After him, perhaps, would be Wolfar, but a long way back.''

''Wolfar?'' Gerin was amazed. ''You can't mean it?''

''Aye, I do. I know of your trouble with him, but you can't deny he's a doughty warrior, and he's not as slow of wit as his looks would make you think.''

''He's a mean one, though. Once in hand-to-hand he almost bit my ear off.'' Something else occurred to the Fox. ''What of your daughter? If the choice were hers, whom would she pick?''

It was Ricolf's turn for surprise. ''What does that matter? She'll do as I bid her.'' He turned back to his archery.

Gerin was tempted to leave but knew his old friend would think him rude to vanish on the eve of the betrothal. He spent the day relaxing, glancing through the few books Ricolf owned, making light talk with a few of the suitors. Van emerged in the early afternoon, a smile on his face. The outlander was rubbing a callus on his right forefinger when he found Gerin, and the baron remembered he was proud of the heavy silver ring he'd worn there. He explained, ''It's only right to give the lassie something to remember me by.''

''You don't think she's likely to forget.''

''I suppose not,'' Van agreed happily.

A bit before sunset a wandering minstrel appeared outside Ricolf's gate and prayed shelter for the night. The baron granted it on condition that he sing after Elise's betrothal was announced. The minstrel, whose name was Tassilo, agreed at once. ''How not?'' he said. ''After all, 'tis the purpose of a singer to sing.''

51

The evening meal was much as it had been the night before. Tonight, though, Ricolf opened the jugs of wine brought up from the south along with griffin-headed ivory rhytons and eared cups of finest Sithonian ware, beautiful scenes of hunting, drinking, and the deeds of the gods painted under their flaze. Gerin's thrifty soul quailed when he thought of what Ricolf must have spent. Rihwin, who seemed to expect his coming triumph and hadn't tasted his beloved wine in a year, began pouring it down almost faster than he could be served. He held it well at first, regaling his comrades with bits of gossip from the Emperor's court. Though this was a year old, most of it was new to Gerin.

The feasters finished. An expectant hush fell on the hall.

Just as Ricolf began to rise, Rihwin suddenly clambered atop the table. The boards creaked. Voice wine-blurred, Rihwin called out, "Ha, bard! Play me a tune, and make it a lively one!" Tassilo, who had looked at the bottom of his cup more than once himself, struck fiery music from his mandolin, and Rihwin went into a northern dance. Gerin stared at him; he was sure Ricolf would not like this. But Rihwin found his jig too sedate and shifted in midstep to a wild stamping nomad dance.

Ricolf, watching the unmanly performance, looked like a man bathing in hellfire. He had all but beggared himself to provide the best for these men and make his holding as much like the elegant southland as he could. Was this to be his reward?

Then, with a howl, Rihwin stood on his hands and kicked his legs in the air in time to the music.

His toga fell limply about his ears, and he was wearing nothing at all beneath it.

At that spectacle the maids hustled Elise from the hall. Gerin did not quite catch her expression, but thought amusement a large part of it.

In agony, Ricolf cried, "Rihwin, you have danced your wife away!"

"I could hardly care less," Rihwin retorted cheerfully. "Play on, minstrel!"

chapter 3

After that there was little enough Ricolf could do. He tried to make the best of the fiasco by proclaiming to everyone that Wolfar of the Axe was his true choice as Elise's groom. Wolfar acknowledged his honor with a gracious growl, which only disconcerted Ricolf more. There were scattered cheers, including a sardonic one from the sodden Rihwin.

Gerin muttered insincere congratulations to Wolfar, then left the feast, claiming he wanted an early start in the morning. There was just enough truth in that to make mannerly his escape from his enemy's victory. Van had already disappeared with another wench and a jug of wine. Ignoring the raucous celebration in the great hall, Gerin blew out the little flame flickering from the middle fingertip of the hand-shaped clay lamp by his bed and was asleep at once.

He woke to the sound of someone fumbling at the barred door. Elleb's crescent, just now topping the walls of Ricolf's keep, peeped through the east-facing slit window and sent a pale pink stripe of light across the bed to the door; sunrise was still two or three hours away Head aching, Gerin groped for his clothes. He slid into his trousers, but wrapped his tunic round his right arm to serve as a shield. The fumbling went on. Knife in hand, he padded to the door and flung it open.

Whatever outcry he had intened clogged in his throat. "Great Dyaus, Elise, what are you dong here?" he gurgled. He almost had not known her. No longer was she gowned and bedecked; she wore stout boots, breeches, and a sheepskin jacket so baggy it all but hid her curves. A knife swung at her belt, and her long hair was tucked up under a shapeless leather traveler's hat.

For a long moment she stared at the blade in his left hand its nicked edge glittering in the fading light of the hallway torches. Then she brushed past the stunned Fox and shut the door behind them. Voice low and fast, she said, "I need help, and of all the men here I think I can only ask it of you, Lord Gerin. I was willing to try my father's idiot scheme as long as I thought I'd have some chance of getting a husband I could endure, but Wolfar of the Axe—"

Gerin wished he had not drunk so much; his head still buzzed and his wits were slow. "All the northland knows I have no love for Wolfar, but what do you want of me?" he asked, already afraid he knew the answer.

She looked up at him, eyes enormous in the gloom. "I know you are going to the City—take me with you! My mother was of a southern house, and I have kin there. I'd be no burden to you; I've been daughter and son both to my father, and I can live from the land like any warrior—"

"Don't you see it's something I can't do?"

55

Gerin broke in. "It's impossible. What would my life be worth if someone were to find you here even now?" Alarmed at that thought, he added, "By the gods, where are your maids?"

"As soon as I knew my father had chosen Wolfar, I put a sleeping powder in their cups. The ninnies were still clucking over poor besotted Rihwin. He wasn't a bad fellow, for all his silly ways."

The baron felt a touch of annoyance at her mentioning the drunken fool with kindness, but stifled it. He said, "There's one for you, then. But why would Ricolf not think I ran off with you against your will?"

"Nothing simpler: I left a note in my room saying just what I was doing, and why. There are things in it only he and I know; he'd not think it forced from me."

Gerin stared. Women who read and wrote were not of the ordinary sort. Well, he thought, I've already found that out. But he shook his head, saying, "You have all the answers, it seems. But answer me this: would you have me break the sacred oath of guest-friendship I hold with your father? No luck comes to the oathbreaker; gods and men alike turn from him."

She inspected him, and he felt himself flinch under her gaze. "You've forgotten the oath you gave me all those years ago, then?" she asked bitterly, and her eyes filled with unshed tears. "How old was I? Eight? Ten? I don't know, but I've remembered from then till now that you treated me as if I was a real person, not just a brat underfoot. You swore if ever I needed you, there would you be. Is an oath less an oath because given to a child? Am I less a person because I have no beard? You called on Dyaus; by Dyaus, Lord Gerin, could you see yourself wed to Wolfar, were you a woman?'' The tears slid down her cheek.

"No," he sighed, understanding what the truth meant but unable to lie to her.

"No more could I. I would sooner die."

"There's no need of that," he said, awkwardly patting her shoulder. He tossed the rolled-up tunic aside and climbed into his cuirass. "What sort of gear do you have?" he asked.

"No need to worry about that; I've already stowed it in your wagon."

He threw his hands in the air. "I might have known. You know, Van will call me nine different kinds of fool, and every one of them true, but you'll be useful to have around; you could talk a longtooth into eating parsnips. Wait here," he added, and stepped into the hall. He tried Van's door and found it barred; he swore under his breath. He was about to tap when the door flew open. Van loomed over him, naked as the day he was born; his mace checked its downward arc inches from Fox's head.

"Captain, what in the five hells are you up to?" he hissed. Behind him the voice of a woman made drowsy complaint; in the half-light the curve of her hip and thigh was an inviting shadow. "It's all right, love," the outlander reassured her. She sighed and went back to sleep. Van turned to Gerin: "Don't ever come scratching round my door. It isn't healthy."

"So I see. Now will you put that fornicating thing down and listen to me?"

When the baron's tale was done, there was nothing but astonishment on Van's face. He

57

whistled softly. "I will be damned," he said. "Spend two years thinking a man stodgy and then he does this to you." His shoulders shook with suppressed mirth. "What are you standing here gawking for? Go on, get the horses hitched up; I'll be with you in a few minutes." Softly but firmly, he shut the door in Gerin's face.

Blinking, the baron retrieved Elise and hurried down the hallway. The only sounds were faint cracklings from the guttering torches and snores from behind almost every door. Gerin thanked the gods for the flooring of rammed earth; on planking the nails in his sandals would have clicked like the wooden snappers some Sithonian dancers wore on their fingers.

"How can I thank you?" Elise whispered. "I—" Gerin clamped a hand over her mouth: someone else was in the hall.

Wolfar, stumbling to his bed, had rarely felt better in his life. He had spent most of the night thinking of Gerin chopped into dogmeat after he took over Ricolf's lands as well as his own, and Elise was a tasty baggage, too. Every other feaster had long since either lurched off to bed or slid under the table, but Wolfar, buoyed by his visions of glory and mayhem, was still mostly himself after drinking them all down. He gaped when Gerin appeared before him.

"Ah, the Fox," he said jovially. "I was just thinking of you." His piggy eyes went wide when he saw the baron's companion.

Gerin saw him fill his lungs to shout. He snatched a dead torch from its dragon-headed bronze sconce and broke it over Wolfar's bald spot. Wolfar sank to the ground without a sound,

58

mouth still open. Gerin and Elise darted for the stables, not knowing how long he would be stunned.

Once outside the castle they slowed; to attract the attention of the gate crew was the last thing they wanted.

The horses looked resentful as Gerin harnessed them. His fingers flew over the leather straps, for at any moment he expected an alarm to sound. But the horses were hitched and Elise hidden under blankets in the back of the wagon, and still all was quiet. There was no sign of Van, either; Gerin waited and worried.

A footfall in the doorway made him whirl, hand leaping for his swordhilt, but that gigantic silhouette could only belong to one man. "What kept you?" the baron barked.

"Captain," Van said with dignity, "there are some things a gentleman never hurries. You laid out Wolfar cold as a cod; he'll have a headache for a week. Now let's be off, shall we? Ah, you've already got a torch lit. Good; here, start another. The light may keep the worst of the ghosts away. Or, of course," he added fatalistically, "it may not. I know few men who've gone night-faring, and fewer still who came back again, but now it's a needful thing."

He climbed aboard, took the reins, and clucked the horses into motion. Harness jingling, they rode up to the gate. A couple of Ricolf's hounds sniffed about the wagon's wheels, but Van flicked them away with his whip.

The gate-guards made no move to let down the drawbridge, but looked curiously at Van and Gerin. One asked, "Lords, why are you on your

59

way so early?''

Van stopped breathing; it was a question for which he had no good answer. But Gerin only grinned a lopsided grin. He laughed at the guard and said, ''I'm running away with Ricolf's daughter; she's much too good for anyone here.''

The soldier shook his head. ''Ask a question like that and you deserve whatever answer you get, I suppose. Come on, Vukov,'' he said to the other watchman, ''let down the bridge. If they want to take their chances with the ghosts, it's their affair and none of mine.'' Smothering a yawn, Vukov helped his comrade with the winch. The bridge lowered slowly, then dropped the last few feet with a thump. To Gerin the clop of the horses' hooves on it seemed the loudest thing in the world.

Trying not to bellow laughter, Van wheezed and choked. Between splutters he managed to say, ''Captain, that was the most outrageous thing I've ever seen in my life! You've got to promise me you'll never, ever let me gamble with you. I have better things to do than throw my money away.''

''It's ill-done to lie in the house of a guest-friend. If his men choose not to believe, why, that's their affair and none of mine,'' Gerin shrugged, mimicking the guardsman.

As soon as they left the shelter of Ricolf's keep the ghosts were at them, keening their loss and shrieking cold resentment of any who still kept warm blood in their veins. Without the boon of blood to placate them, they sent an icy blast of terror down on the travelers. The horses rolled their eyes, shying at things only they saw. Gerin stopped his ears with his fingers in a vain effort to shut out the ghosts' wails. He saw Van work his massive

60

jaw, but no word of complaint passed the outlander's lips. Elise, shivering, came up to sit with them under the scant protection the torches gave.

Ricolf's lands shot by in a gray blur, as if Van thought to outrun the ghosts by fleeing south. The horses did not falter, but seemed glad to run. False dawn was touching the east with yellow light when the wagon sped past the little guardpost Ricolf kept on his southern border. Gerin was not much surprised to see the guards curled up asleep inside; fire and blood warded them from the night spirits. They did not stir when the wagon went by.

Half expecting pursuit, the Fox had been looking back over his shoulder as long as he was in Ricolf's lands. When he saw how much Van slowed his pace once past the border he knew he had not been alone. He cocked an eyebrow at his friend. "For all his willingness to help carry off the lady," he said to no-one in particular, "I seem to notice a certain burly accomplice of mine lacking a perfect faith in the power of her notes to soothe ruffled tempers."

"If all that noise means me," Van rumbled, "then you've hit in the center of the target. It would have been downright awkward to have to explain to a horde of warriors just what I was doing with their lord's daughter."

Elise made a face at him. She, at least, seemed confident there would be no followers. Gerin wondered what it took to put trust in someone unknown for a double handful of years. His mind stalked round the idea like a cat with ruffled fur, and he was still astonished any pleading of Elise's could have convinced him to bring her along.

At last the sun touched the eastern horizon, spilling out ruddy light like a huge hand pouring wine from a jug. The ghosts gave a last frightened moan and returned to whatever gloomy haunts they inhabited during the day.

The morning wore on with no sign of anyone on their trail, but Gerin still felt uneasy for no reason he could name. It could not have been the land; save for the High Kirs, now a deep blue shadow on the southern skyline, there was nothing to be seen much different than he knew in his own barony. Meadow and forest alternated, and if there were a few more elms and oaks and a few less pines and maples, that mattered little. The woods did grow closer to the road than the Fox would have liked: south of Ricolf's holding the highway marked the boundaries of two barons said to be rivals, and to Gerin's way of thinking they should have kept the undergrowth well trimmed so it could not be used for cover.

Once a little stream wound close by the roadway. When Van pulled off to water the horses and let them rest for a few minutes, frogs and turtles leaped from mossy rocks and churned away in senseless terror, just as they would have done near Fox Keep. No, the Fox thought as he stared back at a suspicious turtle, the land was not what troubled him.

The peasants seemed much the same, too. The lived in little villages of wattle and daub, the community oxen housed about as well as the people. Scrawny chickens picked around their cottages and squawked warnings at their dogs, who snarled back. Little naked herdboys guided their flocks of sheep and cattle with sticks, helped by the short-legged brown and white dogs native to the north country. Men and women in colorless homespun worked in the fields, knowing no less toil than the draft animals laboring with them.

Not until Gerin lifted his eyes to the keep could he finger what was troubling him. Castles crowned many hills, but here and there the banks of their moats were beginning to crumble into the water. Some lesser barons let stands of trees big enough to shelter scores of warriors grow almost within bowshot of their walls. Gerin had no desire to claim shelter from any of these nobles. The few he saw on the road distressed him. Their chariots were decorated with inlays of gold and bright stones, but they plainly had never seen combat. More than one man wore cloth instead of mail, and what cuirasses were to be seen were covered with studs and curlicues of bronze: beautiful to look at but sure to catch and hold a spearpoint. The footsoldiers were not much better. They were well armed, but soft jaws and thick middles said these were unblooded troops. Behind the shield of the border, where the Trokmoi were always ready to pounce on the weak, Elabon's northern province was starting to rot.

Van saw it too. "This land is ripe for the taking," he said, and Gerin could do nothing but nod.

The sun rose high and hot. Gerin felt the sweat trickle down his back and chest and wished he could scratch through his armor. With his fairer skin Van suffered more, tanned though he was. He finally took off his proud helm and stowed it carefully in the back of the wagon, then poured over his head a bucket of cool water from the brook where they had stopped. He puffed and

63

snorted as the water poured down his face and dripped through his beard. "Ahhh!" he said. "That's better, even if I do sound like a whale coming up for air."

"A whale?" Elise asked. She had shed her jacket, and in tunic and trousers was more comfortable than either of the men. Her hat she kept on, for her fairness was not like that of Van, who grew golden under the sun: she would burn and freckle and peel and never really become tan at all. She went on, "I've heard the word. Some kind of fish, is it not? But I've never seen one."

"Nor I," Gerin said. "The farthest I've traveled is to the City, and there are no whales in the Inner Seas."

"Well, Captain, I'll tell you—and you, my lady—I've seen whales right enough, and closer than I wanted, too. Do you know the land called Mabalal?"

Elise shook her head. Gerin said, "I've heard the name. It's far to the south and east, I think."

"That's the one, Captain. And sultry—why, this is nothing beside what it's like there! I thought I'd melt like a lump of wax in a fire. The people there are little and dark, and they seem to like it well enough. For all their swarthy hides, though, the women are not uncomely, and what they do—" Van broke off abruptly, and Gerin was amused to see that his huge friend could blush.

"But I was talking about whales," Van went on. "They come in all sizes, and the sailors like the little ones, and wouldn't think of harming them. But the big ones hate men and sink whatever boats they can. Now, one of them had lived outside the harbor at Jalor—that's the capital thereabouts—for

64

years, and he'd sunk maybe twenty ships. He had a reddish skin they knew him by, and they called him 'Old Crimson,' since crimson is the color their kings wear. Five times they'd tried to kill him, and neither of the two harpooners who lived was whole.

"It got so bad the captains wouldn't ship out of Jalor, and if they did they couldn't find a soul to man the oars. Didn't that put a pretty squeeze on the merchants! So they decided to have another go at him, and when one of their big traders, a fellow named Kariri, saw me in some dive, he thought I would make a good oarsman, having more in the way of muscle than his countrymen. I was game; things had been dull since I'd had to leave Shanda, and the price he promised was good. It had to be, to get rowers for that boat! Most of us were foreigners of one kind or another: the folk of Jalor knew better.

"So off we sailed, the only ship in the water, though the docks and beach were black with people watching. Now, in those parts the way they lure whales is this: they catch a lot of fat tunny and pickle them with salt in big jars, and when they're nice and ripe, they soak rags in the fish-grease and dump 'em in the water where they think the whales are. The whales can scent this grease a long way off, and follow it to the boat. The first thing any of us knew of Old Crimson being round was a sort of a loud hiss and a cloud of evil-smelling steam. Whales aren't like other fish; they have to come to the surface every so often to get a breath of air and blow out the old. That's what he'd done, not fifty yards to starboard.

"I tell you, I missed a stroke, and I wasn't the

65

only one. Then he came all the way out of the water, and I never want to see such a sight again. That ruddy hide of his was all scarred and torn from the ships he'd sunk, and I saw three spearpoints stuck in just back of his head, but not deep enough to do more than drive him mad with pain over the years. I don't lie when I say I'd sooner have been elsewhere right then. He was bigger than our boat, and not by a little, either.

"But the harpooning crew knew what to do if they—and we—were going to come home alive. They tossed ten or twelve pounds of that pickled tunny toward the monster, and he snapped it up. It's a funny thing, but the stuff makes whales drunk, and Old Crimson lay still in the water. If he were a kitten, he would have purred.

"Once that happened, the harpooners slipped out of their clothes (not that they wore much, just rags round their middles) and swam over to him as quiet as they could. One trailed his barbed harpoon, the second a little stand for it, and the third, who had more brawn than most men of Mabalal, took a big mallet with him. They climbed up on Old Crimson's head, and he never stirred. We lay dead quiet in the water for fear of rousing him.

"They set up the harpoon just aft of his head, right behind the others that hadn't gone deep enough to kill. Then the fellow with the mallet swung it up over his head and hit the butt end of the harpoon with everything he had. I swear by all the gods there are that the whale leaped clean out of the water, with the harpooners still clinging to him. They might have screamed, but we never would have heard them. We were backing water for all we were worth, but still I saw that great tail

66

like a fist over the bow. When it came down the ship just went all to splinters. I'm hazy about what happened next, because something hit me right between the eyes. I must have grabbed an oar; the next thing I remember is being fished out of the water by one of the little boats that came out as soon as the people on shore saw Old Crimson was really dead. Thirty-four people were on our boat when we set out, and six of us lived. Anyway, the fishermen who rescued me took me to shore, and the Jalorians took the whale's carcass ashore too, for they valued the meat and oil of it. The head of the merchants' guild kissed all of us who had lived, called us the saviors of the town, and gave each of us a tooth worried out of the whale's head: I don't lie when I say it was more than half a foot long.

"But do you know what? I didn't make a copper more from it, for that fat merchant sitting on his arse on the shore just called me a filthy foreigner and wouldn't pay. For all that, though, I drank my way through the grogshops for ten days straight without touching a coin of my own, and to this day no-one in Jalor knows how old Kadiri's warehouses burnt down."

"You know," Gerin said thoughtfully, "if they were to put a line on the end of their harpoons with floats—sealed empty casks, maybe—every hundred paces or so, they could spear their whales without having to climb onto them, and if the wound didn't kill on the spot, the whales couldn't escape by diving, either."

Van stared at him. "I do believe it'd work," he said at last. "Why weren't you there then to think of it? The gods know I never would have." He looked at Elise. "Gerin, I do believe our guests

67

thinks my yarn would be good for making flowers grow, but not much else, though since she's kind as she is fair she's too polite to say so. Hold the reins a bit for me, will you?''

Elise started to protest, but Van was not listening to her. He stepped into the back of the wagon; Gerin heard him rummaging in the battered leather sack where he kept his treasures. After a minute or two he grunted in satisfaction and emerged, handing what he held to Elise.

Gerin craned his neck to look too. It was an ivory tusk unlike any he had ever seen: though no longer than the fangs of the longtooth he knew, this was twice as thick and pure white, not yellowish. Someone had carved a whale and the prow of an unfamiliar ship on the tooth; the whale was tinted a delicate pink. Seeing the baron's admiration, Van said, ''A friend of mine made it while I was out roistering. You'll notice it isn't done, but I was in a hurry when I left Jalor, and he didn't have time to finish.''

Elise was silent.

Gerin kept the reins; Van had been yawning all morning, and now he tried to snatch some sleep in the cramped rear of the wagon. The Fox was looking for one particular dirt track of the many joining the Elabon Way. Each path had a stone post set beside it, carved with the marks of the petty barons to whose keeps the roadlets ran. It was past noon before Gerin saw the winged eye he sought. He almost passed it by, for the carving was so ancient that parts of it had weathered away, and startling red lichens covered much of what remained.

"Where are we going?" Elise asked when he turned down the track. She coughed as the horses kicked up dust.

"I thought you'd heard all my plans," Gerin said. "I'd like to hear what the Sibyl at Ikos may tell me. I stopped there once before, when I went south for the first time, and she warned me I'd never be a scholar. I laughed at her, but two years later the Trokmoi killed my father and my brother and I had to quit the southlands."

"That I had heard," Elise said softly. "I'm sorry." It was no conventional expression of regret; Gerin could feel the truth in her words. He was touched, and at the same time half-annoyed with himself for letting her sympathy reach him. He was a bit relieved when she returned to her original thought: "Where we go matters little to me: I simply did not know. Any place away from Wolfar is good enough, though I've heard evil things of the country round Ikos."

"I've heard them too," he admitted, "but I've never seen much to make me think them true. This road goes through some of the deepest forest on this side of the Niffet and over the hills ahead before it reaches the Sibyl's shrine. It's said strange beasts dwell in the forest, but I never saw any, though there were tracks on the roadway that belong to no animals the outer world knows."

The more prosperous petty barons and their lands clung leechlike to the Elabon Way. A few hours' travel from it things were poorer. Freeholders owned their own plots, men not under the dominion of any local lordling. They were of an ancient race, the fold who had held the land

69

between the Niffet and the High Kirs even before the coming of the Trokmoi whom the Empire had expelled. Slim and dark, they spoke the tongue of Elabon fluently enough, but among themselves used their own soft, sibilant language.

The road narrowed, becoming little more than a winding rutted lane under frowning trees. The sinking sun's light could barely reach through the green arcade overhead, and Gerin jumped when a scarlet finch shot across the roadway, taken aback by the flash of color in the gloom. As the sun set he pulled off the road and behind a thick clump of trees. He routed Van from his jouncing bed; together they unharnessed the horses and let them crop what little grass grew in the shade of the tall beeches.

They had but a scanty offering for the ghosts: dried beef mixed with water. It was not really enough, but Gerin hoped it would serve. Elise wanted to take one watch; the baron and Van said no in the same breath.

"Please yourselves," she shrugged, "but I could do it well enough." A knife appeared in her hand and then, almost before the eye could see it, was quivering in a tree trunk twenty feet away.

Gerin was thoughtful as he plucked the dagger free, but still refused. Elise cast an appealing glance at Van. He shook his head and laughed, "My lady, I haven't been guarded by women since I was old enough to keep my mother from learning what I was up to, and I don't plan to start over now."

She looked hurt, but said only, "Very well, then. Guard me well this night, heroes." She half-sketched a salute as she slipped into her bedroll.

70

Van, who was rested, offered to take the first watch. Gerin shrugged himself under a blanket, twisted until he found a position where no pebbles dug into him, and knew nothing more until Van prodded him awake. "Math is down, and—what do you call the fast moon? I've clean forgotten."

"Tiwaz."

"That's it. As well as I can see through the trees, it'll set in an hour or so. That makes it midnight, and time for me to sleep." Van was under his own blanket—the gold-and-black striped hide of some great hunting beast—and asleep with the speed of the true traveler. Gerin stretched, yawned, and heard the ghosts buzz in his mind like gnats.

In the dim red light of the embers the wagon was a lump on the edge of visibility, the horses a pair of dark shadows. Gerin listened to their unhurried breathing and the chirp and rustle of tiny crawling things. An owl overhead loosed its hollow, eerie call. Somewhere not far away a tiny stream chuckled to itself. In the distance a longtooth roared, and for a moment everything else was quiet.

The baron turned at a sound close by. He saw Elise half-sitting, watching him. Her expression was unreadable. "Regrets?" he asked, voice the barest thread of sound.

Her answer was softer still. "Of course. To leave all I've ever known . . . it's no easy road, but one I have to travel."

"You could still go back."

"With Wolfar's arms waiting there's no returning." She started to say more, stopped, then began again. "Do you know why I came with you? You helped me once before, long ago." Her eyes were

71

looking into the past, not at Gerin. "The first time I saw you was the most woeful day of my life. I had a dog I'd raised from a pup; he had a floppy ear and one of his eyes was half blue, and because of his red fur I called him Elleb. He used to like to go out and hunt rabbits, and when he caught one he'd bring it home to me. One day he went out like he always did, but he didn't come back.

"I was frantic. I looked for two days before I could find him, and when I did I wished I hadn't. He'd run down a little gully and caught his hind leg in a trap."

"I remember," Gerin said, realizing why the dog Ruffian had seemed familiar. "I heard you crying and went to see what the trouble was. I was heading south to study."

"Was I crying? I suppose I was, but I don't remember. All I can think of is poor Elleb's leg shredded in the jaws of the trap, and the blood dried black, and the flies. The trap was chained to a stake, and I couldn't pry it loose from him.

"Hurt as he was, I remember him growling when you came up, still trying to keep me safe. You knelt down beside me and patted him and gave him a little water from your canteen, and then you took out your knife and did what needed to be done.

"Not many would have tried to make friends with him first, and not many would have sat with me afterwards and made me understand why an end to his pain was the last gift he could get from someone who loved him. By the time you'd taken me home I really did understand it. You were kind to me, and I've never forgotten."

"And because of so small a thing you put your

trust in me?''

''I did,'' she answered simply, ''and I have no regrets.'' Her last words were sleep-softened.

Gerin watched Nothos and the stars peep through holes in the leafy canopy and thought about the obligations with which he had saddled himself. After a while he decided he too had no regrets. He fed bits of wood to the tiny fire, slapped at the buzzing biters lured by its light, and waited for the sun to put the ghosts to rout.

At dawn he woke Van. His comrade knuckled his eyes and spoke mostly in sleepy grunts as they harnessed the horses. Elise doused and covered the fire before Gerin could tend to it. They breakfasted on hard bread and smoked meat; to his disgust, Gerin missed a shot at a fat grouse foolish enough to roost on a branch not a hundred feet away. It flapped off, wings whirring.

The track wound its way through the forest. Trailing shoots and damp hanging mosses hung from branches overhead, eager to snatch at anything daring to brave the wood's cool dim calm. The horses were balky, and more than once Van had to touch them with the whip before they would go on.

Few birds trilled to ease the quiet; almost the only sounds were the creaking of branches and the rustling of leaves in a breeze too soft to reach down to the road. Once a sound almost softer than silence paced the wagon for a time. It might have been the pad of great supple feet, or perhaps nothing at all. Gerin saw—or thought he saw—a pair of eyes, greener than the leaves, measuring him. He blinked or they blinked and when he looked again they were gone. The rattle of the

73

wagon's wheels was swallowed as if it had never been.

"Place gives me the bloody shivers!" Van said. Gerin thought his friend's voice a bit louder than needful.

The baron thought the day passing faster than it was, so thick was the gloom. He bit back an exclamation of surprise when they burst from the shadows into the brightness of the late afternoon sun. He had not realized how much the thought of again camping in the forest chilled him until he saw it was unnecessary.

The hills cupped the valley in which Ikos lay, letting travelers look down on their goal before they reached it. The main road came from the southwest, and Gerin could see little dots of moving men, carriages, and wagons, all come to consult the Sibyl. His own road was less used. The border lords usually put more faith in edged bronze than prophecy.

The temple itself was surrounded by a tiny grove of trees. Probably in days long past the forest had lapped down from the hilltops into the valley, but the sacred grove was the only trace of it. The shrine's glistening marble roof stood out vividly against the green of the trees. Around the temple proper were the houses of the priests, the attendants, and the little people who, while not really connected with the Sibyl, made their livings from those who came to see her: sellers of images and sacrificial animals, free-lance soothsayers and oracle-interpreters, innkeepers and whores, and the motley crew who sold amulets, charms, and doubtless curses, too.

Around the townlet were cleared fields, each small plot owned by a freeholder. Gerin knew the temple clung to its old ways and did not grudge it its customs, but still thought freeholding subversive. There was no way for a peasant to produce enough wealth to be able to equip himself with all the gear a proper warrior needed, and without the nobles the border and all the land behind would be a red tangle of warfare, with the barbarians howling down to loot and burn and kill.

"Should we go down before the light fails?" Van asked.

Gerin thought of Ikos' dingy hostels and shook his head. "We'd get nothing done at this hour, and from what I recall of the inns, there will be fewer bugs here."

The evening meal was spare, taken from the same rations as breakfast. Gerin knew those had been packed with the idea of feeding two people, not three, and reminded himself to lay in more. Pretty sorry scholar you are, he jeered at himself, worrying over smoked sausages and journeybread.

He must have said that aloud, for Van laughed and answered, "Well, Captain, someone has to do it, after all."

The baron took the first watch. In Ikos below the lights faded until all was dark save for a central watchfire. The town watchman cast a huge flickering shadow as he paced about. The hills to the southwest were dotted with tiny patches of light Gerin knew to be camps like his own. In its grove, the temple was strange, for the light streaming out from it glowed blue instead of the comfortable red-gold of honest flame.

Magic, Gerin decided sleepily, or else the god was walking about inside. When Math's golden half-circle set he woke Van, then dove headfirst into sleep.

He woke to the scent of cooking; luckier than he had been the morning before, Van had bagged a squirrel and two rabbits and was stewing them. Elise contributed mushrooms and a handful of herbs. Feeling much better about the world now that his belly was full, Gerin hitched up the horses and the wagon rolled down the path toward the Sibyl.

chapter 4

It was not long before he discovered his memory had buried a great deal when it came to Ikos. First of all, the place stank. It lay under a cloud of incense so cloying that Gerin wished he could stow his nose in the wagon. Mixed with the sweet reek was the scent of charring fat from the sacrifices, as well as the usual town odors of stale cookery, garbage, ordure, and long-unwashed animals and humanity.

The noise was every bit as bad. Gerin's ears had not faced such an assault since he returned to the north country. It seemed as if every peddler in Ikos rolled down on the wagon, each crying his wares at something more than the top of his lungs: sword-blades, rare and potent drugs, sanctified water, oats, pretty boys, savory cooked geese, collected books of prophetic verse, and countless other things. A fat bald man in greasy tunic and shiny leather apron, plainly an innkeeper from the look of him, pushed his way through the press and bowed low before a bemused Gerin, who had never seen him before. "Count Stoffer, I believe?" he asked, back still bent.

Patience utterly exhausted, the Fox snapped, "Well, if you believe that, you'll believe anything, won't you?" and left the poor fellow to the jeers of his fellow-townsmen.

"Is this what the City is like?" Elise asked faintly.

"It is," Gerin said, "but only if you will allow that a map is like the country it pictures."

She used a word he had not suspected young girls knew.

Van chuckled and said, "It's the same problem both places, I think: too many people all pushed together. Captain, you're the only one of us with pockets. Have a care they aren't slit."

Gerin thumped himself to make sure he was still secure. "If any of these fine bucks tries it, he'll be slit himself, and not in the pocket."

They pushed their slow way through the swarming town of Ikos and into the clearing round the sacred grove. The sun was already high when they reached it, and they bought cheese and little bowls of barley porridge from the legion of venders. Men from every nation Gerin knew cursed and jostled one another, each trying to be the first to the god's voice on earth.

One lightly-built chariot held a brace of nomads from the plains of the east. They were little and lithe, flat of face and dark of skin, with scraggly charicatures of beards dangling from their chins. They dressed in wolfskin jackets and leather trousers, and bore double-curved bows reinforced with sinew. They carried small leather shields on their left arms; one was bossed with a golden panther, the other with a leaping stag. When Van noticed them he shouted something in a language that sounded like hissing snakes. Their slanted eyes lit up as they gave eager answer.

There were Kizzuwatnans in heavy carts hauled by straining donkeys: squat, heavy-boned men with swarthy skins, broad, hook-nosed faces, and liquid, mournful eyes. Their hair and beards curled in ringlets, and they wore long linen tunics that reached their knees.

There were a few Sithonians, though most of them preferred the oracle at Pronni in their own country. Slimmer and fairer than the Kizzuwatnans, they wore woolen mantles with brightly-dyed edgings. They peered about scornfully from under their broad-brimmed straw hats: though they had been subjects of the Empire for five centuries, they still saw themselves as something of an elite, and looked down on their Elabonian overlords as muscular dullards.

Even an Urfa from the deserts of the farthest south had come to Ikos. He must have ridden all the way around Elabon's Greater Inner Sea, for he was still perched atop his camel. Gerin looked at its harness with interest, thinking how fascinated Duin would have been. The desert-dweller looked down at the wains and chariots around him, and growled guttural warning when they came too close. That was seldom; horses shied away from his evil-looking mount. The Urfa was wrapped in a robe of grimy wool. Eyes and teeth flashed in a face blackened by dirt and long years of sun. Save for a nose even larger than the Kizzuwatnans', his features were delicate, almost feminine. He wore a thin fringe of beard and, for all his filth, seemed to think himself the lord of creation.

Gerin had a hard time putting names to some of

the other outlanders. Van claimed one black-haired, fair-skinned giant belonged to the Gradi, who lived to the north of the Trokmoi. The man was afoot, and sweating in his furs. He carried a stout mace and a short-handled throwing axe. Of the Gradi Gerin knew almost nothing, but Van spoke of them with casual familiarity.

"Do your know their tongue?" Elise asked.

"Aye, a bit."

"Just how many languages do you know?" Gerin wondered.

"Well, if you mean to say hello in, and maybe swear a bit, gods, I've lost track long since. Tongues I know fairly well, though, perhaps ten or a dozen. Something like that."

"Which of them is your own?" Elise asked him.

"My lady," Van said, with something as close to embarrassment as his deep voice could produce, "I've been on the road for a lot of years now. After a bit of time it matters little where I started."

Gerin grinned wryly: he'd had much the same answer when he asked that question. Elise plainly wanted to pursue it further, but held her tongue.

One group of foreigners the Fox knew only too well: the Trokmoi. Three of their chieftains had come to consult the Sibyl, their chariots staying together in the disorder. They were from deep in the northern woods, for Gerin, who knew the clans on the northern side of the border as well as he knew the barons warding it, recognized none of them, nor were the clan patterns of bright checks on their drivers' tunics familiar to him. Chiefs and drivers alike were tall thin men; four had red hair and two were blond. All wore their hair long and

80

had huge drooping mustachios, though they shaved their cheeks and chins. Two clutched jugs of ale to themselves; another wore a necklace of human ears.

Priests circulated through the crowd. Gerin looked with scant liking at the one approaching the wagon. A robe of gold brocade was stretched across his over-ample belly, and his beardless cheeks shone pink. Everything about him was round and soft, from his limpid blue eyes to the toes peeking sausage-like from his sandals. He was a eunuch, for the god accepted no whole men as his servitors.

The tip of his tongue played redly across his lips as he asked, "What would your business be, gentles, with the Sibyl of my Lord Briton?" His voice was soft and sticky, like the caress of a hand dripping with honey.

"I'd sooner not speak of it in public," Gerin said.

"Quite, quite. Your servant Falfarun most definitely agrees. You have, though, a suitably appropriate offering for the god, I hope?"

"I think so," Gerin said, and swung a purse into Falfarun's pudgy fist.

The priest's face was blank. "Doubtless all will be well when your question is heard," he said.

"I do hope, my dear Falfarun," Gerin said in his suavest voice, "it will be heard soon." He handed the priest another, larger, purse, which vanished into a fold of his robe.

"Indeed. Yes, indeed. Come this way, if you please." Falfarun neared briskness as he elbowed aside less forethoughtful seekers of divine wisdom. Clucking to the horses, Van steered after him.

Gerin was conscious of the black looks he was getting, but ignored them. Falfarun led the wagon into the sacred grove around the temple precinct. Seeing the Fox's success, the Trokmoi pulled off rings, armlets, and a heavy golden pectoral and waved them in the face of another plum priest.

"You gauged the size of your second sack about right," Van whispered.

"Praise Dyaus for that! The last time I was here I spent three days cooling my heels before I got so much as a look at the Sibyl. I was still too young to know the world runs on cash."

"Was the wench worth looking at, once you finally saw her?"

"Scarcely. She was a wrinkled old crone. I wonder if she still lives."

"Why have hags to give prophesies? It seems to me they'd hardly be fitting mates for whatever god runs the shrine here. Give me a juicy lass every time," Van added, drawing a sniff from Elise.

"Biton has spoken through her since she was chosen for him when she was still a child," Gerin explained. "Whenever a Sibyl dies the priests search among the families of the old race; this valley has always been their stronghold. When they find a girl-child with a certain mark—what it is they keep secret, but it has been Biton's sign for ages beyond count—she becomes the new Sibyl as long as she remains a maiden: and her chastity is guarded, I assure you."

The tumult behind them faded under the trees. Images of all-seeing Biton were everywhere in the grove, half of them turned to show the two eyes in the back of his head. Another priest was leading the Trokmoi along a different a path; far from

82

being struck by the holiness of the wood, they argued loudly in their own language.

High walls of gleaming white marble warded the outer courtyard of Biton's temple. The gates were flung wide, but spear-carrying temple guardsmen stood ready to slam them shut in seconds should trouble threaten. Here and there the shining stone was chipped and discolored, a mute reminder of the great invasion of the Trokmoi two hundred sixty years before, when Biton himself, the priests maintained, had appeared to drive the barbarians from his shrine.

Before they could go in, Falfarun summoned a green-robed underpriest. The fat priest said, "It is not permitted to enter the courtyard save on foot; Arcarola here will take your wagon to its proper place. Fear not, for there is no theft on the grounds of the temple. A loathsome plague unfailingly smites any miscreant daring to attempt such rapine."

"How many are thus stricken?" Gerin asked skeptically.

The body of the latest is one of the curiosities within the outer walls. Poor wretch, may he edify the others."

Sobered, Gerin descended from the wagon, followed by Elise and Van. When Arcarola climbed up the horses rolled their eyes and tried to rear, feeling the unfamiliar touch at the reins. Van put a heavy hand on each one's muzzle and growled, "Don't be stupid, now," following that with an oath in the harsh tongue Gerin guessed was his own. The beasts subsided and let themselves be led away.

About that time the Trokmoi came up; more

83

green-robes took their chariots away. The priest who was leading them drew Falfarun aside and spoke softly with him. The Trokmoi were talking too, and not softly: the argument they had begun under the trees of the sacred grove was still in full swing. Gerin was about to greet them in their own tongue until he heard what they were quarreling about.

One of the northerners looked suspiciously at the baron and his comrades. "Not so loud should you be making it, Catuvolcus," he said. He sounded worried, and his scarred hands made shushing motions.

Catuvolcus was not going to be hushed. Gerin guessed he was a bit drunk. His eyes were shot with red, and his speech was slurred. He toyed with his gruesome necklace. "Divico," he said, "you can take a flying futter at fast Fomor." He used the northern word for the inner moon. "What's the likelihood we would be finding someone this far south who might be speaking the real language?"

"There's no need to be taking a chance with no purpose."

"But what I'm saying is that it's no chance at all. And if you will be remembering, 'twas your scheme to be coming here. What was the why of it, now? Just to have the privacy we could scarce be getting from our own oracles?"

"And a proper notion it was, too. I'd liefer not have that Balamung omadhaun know it's less than full faith I have in him. Who is the spalpeen, anyhow, and why should we be fighting for him? If I go hunting with a bear, why, I want to be sure he'll not save me for the main course."

Listening as hard as he could without seeming

to, Gerin barely noticed Falfarun's return. He was trailed by the other priest, who was even fatter than he. Falfarun coughed and said, "Good sir, my colleague, Saspir" he indicated his companion, whose smooth eunuch's face belied the years claimed by his graying hair and sagging jowls "and I have decided that these northern gentlemen should precede you to the Sibyl, as their journey has been longer than yours and they have urgent business in their own land, which requires them to make haste."

"You are trying to tell me they have paid you more," Gerin said without much rancor.

Falfarun's chins quivered. His voice was hurt as he answered, "I would not put it so crassly—"

"—But it's still true," Gerin finished for him. "Be it so, then, if we can follow them directly."

"But of course," Falfarun said, relieved to find him so agreeable. Saspir gave the Trokmoi the good news and took them into the courtyard of the temple. Falfarun followed, his reedy voice loud in the ears of Gerin, who would much rather have listened to the barbarians. Another golden-robed hierarch conducted a toga-clad noble from the holy precinct; the man's thin, pale face bore a troubled expression. The nomads from the plains of Shanda came up just as Gerin entered the courtyard, and he heard a priest calmly overriding their loud objections to being separated from their chariot.

Even the Trokmoi fell silent in the temple forecourt; they gawked, necks craning every which way, trying to see everything at once and looking like nothing so much as hungry hounds licking their chops in front of a butchershop. Gerin did

85

not blame them much, for the sight of so much treasure affected him the same way. The would-be thief's corpse, covered with hideous raw-edged lesions and bloated and stinking after some days in the open, did little to dampen his enthusiasm. Beside him Van whistled, soft and low.

Only the gauds were on display; most of the riches Biton's shrine had accumulated over the centuries were stored away in strong-walled vaults behind the temple or in caves below it. What was visible was more than enough to rouse a plunderer's lusts. Chief among the marvels were twin ten-foot statues of gold and ivory, one of the Emperor Oren II, who had built the temple in the ancient grove, the other of his father, Ros the Fierce, who drove the Trokmoi north of the River Niffet and won the lands between the Niffet and the Kirs for Elabon. Oren wore the toga and held in his upraised right hand the orb of empire; Ros, mailed, had a javelin ready to cast and leaned upon a narrow-waisted shield of antique design. His stern, craggy face, with its thrusting nose and lines carved deep on weathered cheeks, still had the power to awe though four hundred years had passed. Gerin shivered when he looked up into those cold eyes of jet. Both images were protected from the elements and the indignities of passing birds by a cloth-of-gold awning and two underpriests armed with long-handled fans.

A huge golden mixing-bowl celebrated Biton's triumph over the Trokmoi. Wider even than Van's outstretched arms, it was set upon a claw-footed tripod of bronze, and held the images of barbarians fleeing the god's just wrath and the prostrate bodies of those his arrows had struck down. On a pedestal of purple marble next to it was a splendid statue of a dying Trokmê. The naked warrior was on his right side, propping himself up with his right arm, its hand still grasping swordhilt. His left hand clutched a gaping gash in his right side; the red-painted blood streamed down his flank to form a puddle at his hip. His face was turned up to stare at his conqueror, and its grimace showed agony and defiance, but not a hint of fear. It's features were blunter than usual among the long-faced, thin-nosed Trokmoi. Probably the sculptor, himself a Sithonian, had used a countryman as a model, adding only long hair and mustaches to make clear the statue's race.

There was much else to see: the silver-and-gold longtooth, its leap onto an aurochs frozen by a master artisan of long ago; the chalices and urns of precious metals, alabaster, cinnabar, and multicolored jades; the stacks of ingots and bars of gold and silver, each with a plaque telling which accurate prophesy it commemorated . . . but Falfaran was conducting them up to the steps of the temple, and that was a sight in itself.

Oren's architect had tried to harmonize the sparely elegant columned shrines the Sithonians loved with the native brickwork fanes of Elabon, and the effort was a noble one. The sides of Biton's shrine were marble blocks; spacious glazed windows helped illuminate the interior. The front wall was pure Sithonian, with its triangular entablature supported by delicately fluted columns of whitest stone, the ends of each drum so perfectly flat no dagger could have found lodging between any two of them. Between architrave and overhanging eaves the frieze, carved by a team of workmen from drawings by the creator of the dying Trokmê, showed Biton, hand outstretched, guiding an imperial column against a disorderly horde of Trokmoi. Ros, harsh features easy to recognize, was in the lead chariot. His men had a kind of tough uniformity in striking contrast to the irregular foe they battled—and also to the barons who came after them.

Up the seven marble steps they went, Falfarun chattering all the while. When Elise heard that statue and frieze sprang from the same man's mind, she asked his name. Falfarun looked shocked and shook his head. "I have no idea," he said. "The work is far too holy to be polluted by such mundanities."

It took Gerin's eyes a few moments to adjust to the inside of the Biton's shrine, accustomed as they were to bright sunshine. They went wide as he saw the splendor within, for its magnificence had faded in his memory.

Limiting himself to simple white stone for the exterior of the building, its designer had let color run riot within. Twin rows of crimson granite columns, polished mirror-bright, led the eye to the altar. That was of sandalwood overlaid with gold and encrusted with all kinds of precious stones, and threw back in coruscating sheets the light cast on it by dozens of fat tapers in three arabesqued silver chandeliers overhead. The temple's inner walls were faced with rare green marble shot with gold; that stone came only from one quarry near Siphnos in Sithonia, and the Fox could but marvel at the sweat and gold needed to haul it here, a journey of several hundred miles over the Greater

Inner Sea and the royal roads of Elabon. Like the columns, it was buffed until it gleamed, and it tinged niche-set gold and silver statues with its own color.

Chanting acolytes paced here and there, intent on Biton's rituals. Their slippers swished over the floor mosaics, their swinging censers filled the air with the fragrances of aloes, myrrh, and other costly incenses. Folk who wanted Biton's aid but needed no sight of the future knelt and prayed in the pews flanking the granite columns. Some kept their heads lowered, others raised them to the ceiling frescoes, as if seeking inspiration from the scenes of the god's begetting by Dyaus on a princess and his subsequent adventures, most of them caused by the jealously of the heavenly queen Darza.

Only in two respects was Biton's shrine unlike many even more superb temples in the lands south of the mountains. One was the image of the god behind the altar; here he was no graceful youth. A square column of rough black stone stood there, drinking in the light and giving back none. Immeasurably old, it could have been a natural pillar save for the faint images of eyes round its top and a jutting phallus stabbing forward from its middle. Biton's priests had only smiled when Oren proclaimed their deity a son of Dyaus; in their hearts they knew whose god was the elder and, seeing that image, Gerin was not inclined to doubt them. Biton's power was rooted in the earth, and in a square of bare earth to the left of the altar was a rift leading down below the roots of the sacred grove to the Sibyl's cave, a rift whose like was unknown in the tamer south.

The Trokmoi were making their obeisances before Biton's altar, the three chieftains on their knees and their drivers flat on their bellies. The rose, dusted themselves off, and followed their guide into the cave's yawning mouth. One of the drivers, a freckled youth with face tight-set against fear, flexed the fingers of hand hand in a sign to avert evil. His other hand was tight on the hilt of his blade.

Falfarun brought up his charges to take the barbarians' place. All bent the knee before Biton, Falfarun panting as he eased his bulk to the floor. Gerin looked up at the dateless idol; for an instant he thought he saw eyes as brown as his own looking back at him, but when he looked again they were only scratches on stone.

Rising, Falfaran asked, "Would it please you to take more comfortable seats while waiting to meet the Sibyl?" Gerin lowered himself into the foremost pew. He ignored the puffing Falfaran, who dabbed at his forehead with a square of blue silk. His thoughts were on the Trokmoi: if these barbarians, men from so deep in the forests he knew nothing of them, had allied their clans with Balamung, how many more had done the same? Fox Keep, it seemed, was in the way of an onslaught more terrible than the attack whose scars still showed on the forecourt's walls, and had not much more chance of standing than battlements of sand against the flowing tide.

He grew more and more jittery until the Trokmoi finally emerged from the cavemouth. They had no liking for what they had heard; all were grim-faced and the young driver who had made the wardsign was white as a temple column, the freckles on his nose and cheeks standing out like splatters of dried blood.

The two chief who had been quarreling outside the temple forecourt were still at it. Divico, even more worried than before, waved a hand in Catuvolcus' face. "Is it not glad you are now we came?" he asked. "Plain as day the witch-woman told us there'd be nought but a fox gnawing at our middles if we join Balamung, plain as day."

"Ox ordure," Catuvolcus said. "The old gammer has no more wits than teeth, the count of which is none. On all the border there's but one southron called the Fox, and were you not listening when himself told us the kern'd be ravens' meat in no more days? It must be done by now, so where's your worry?"

Gerin stood and gave the Trokmoi his politest bow. "Begging your pardons," he said, using their tongue with a borderer's ease, "but a wizard's word's a coin I'd bite or ever I pocketed it. But if you're after seeking the Fox, it's him I am, and I tell you this: the raven who'll pick my bones is not yet hatched, no, nor his grandfather either."

He had hoped his sudden appearance would show the barbarians the folly of their ways, but instead he saw the rashness of his, for Catuvolcus bellowed an oath, rasped sword from scabbard, and rushed, followed close by his five comrades.

Leaping to his feet, Van heaved Falfarun over his head as easily as if the fat eunuch had been stuffed with down. He pitched him into the Trokmoi, bowling over two of them and giving himself and Gerin time to free their blades. At the same instant Elise hurled a dagger and skipped back to safety. The freckled driver fell, his throat

91

pumping a torrent of blood round the hilt suddenly flowering there and his brand slipping from nerveless fingers.

Catuvolcus ducked under the hurtling priest, swung up his two-handed sword, and brought it down in a cut to cleave Gerin from crown to chin. Sparks flew as the Fox blocked the stroke; his arm felt numb to the elbow. He ducked under another wild slash, edged bronze whizzing bare inches above his head. His own sword leaped forth, biting into the Trokmê's belly; he ripped it free to parry the lunge of one of the drivers. The northerner seemed confused at facing a lefthanded swordsman. Gerin beat down another tentative thrust, feinted at his enemy's throat, and guided his sword into the barbarian's heart. More surprise than pain on his face, the Trokmê swayed and fell. He gasped for the air he could not breathe and tried to speak, but only blood gushed from between his lips.

The Fox cleared his sword and looked around for more fight, but there was none. Van leaned on his blade and puffed, watching the shrilling, scrambling eunuchs with distaste. Half the proud crest of his helm was sheared away and his armor was drenched in gore, but none was his. Red hair matted by redder blood, the head of one barbarian stared glassily at its body. The ghastly corpse lay atop another, whose entrails and pouring blood befouled the gentle meadow of the mosaic floor.

A look of horror on her face, Elise came up to survey the carnage. With a flourish Van plucked her dagger from its victim's throat and handed the dripping weapon to her. "As fine a throw as ever I've seen, and as timely, too," he said. She held it

92

for a moment, then threw it to the floor as hard as she could and gagged, reeling back against the pews.

Gerin put a hand on her shoulder to comfort her; she clung to him and sobbed. He murmured wordless reassurances. He was nearly as much an accidental warrior as was she, and recalled only too well puking up his guts in a clump of bushes after his first kill. Now he felt only gladness that he was still among the living and tried not to think of the ruined humanity at his feet.

He offered his canteen to Elise so she could rinse her mouth. She took it with a muffled word of thanks.

A squad of temple guardsmen rushed down the main aisle, brushing aside the plainsmen (who had watched the fight with interest) and their guide. The guard captain, his cuirass gilded to show his rank, shook his head when he heard Gerin's story, even though Saspir confirmed it. Tugging at his beard, the officer, whose name was Etchebar, said, "To slay a priest of the god, even to save your own lives, is foully done. Surprised am I Briton did not smite you dead."

"Slay?" Van shouted. "Who in the five hells said anything about slaying a priest, you jounce-brained lump of dung?" Etchebar's spearmen bristled at that, but restrained themselves at his gesture. "The great tun is no more slain than you, as you'll find if you flip water in his fat face. Likely less—if we'd waited for your aid, it'd be the Trokmoi you were jabbering with here!" He spat into a pool of red. "Look!" As smoothly as before, he lifted Falfarun from the inert Divico, whom he still covered, and set the priest on his

93

feet, blood dribbling from the hem of his robe. Van slapped him gently once or twice. He groaned and clutched his head but did not seem hurt, however shaken he was.

Gerin turned all his powers of persuasion on the guard captain and the priest, who had one eye already beginning to blacken. He broke off in mid-sentence when he saw Van stooping over Divico, plainly intending to finish off the unconscious man. He made a quick grab for his friend's arm. "Captain, are you daft?" Van demanded.

"I hope not." Gerin took Van's place over the fallen Trokmê and shook him.

Divico came to himself with a thunderstorm in his head. He groaned and opened his eyes; that accursed Fox was bending over him, the scar over his eye white against his tan and his square face hard. The Trokmê gathered himself for a spring and felt the cold kiss of a blade at his throat. He rolled his eyes down until he could see its upper edge, still smeared with blood. Impotent rage flashed across his face. "I willna beg for my life, if it's that you're after," he said. "Slit my weasand and have done."

"A warrior's answer," Gerin nodded, still speaking in the forest tongue with a fluency Divico found damnable. "Can it be you're wise as well?" He sheathed his sword and helped the bewildered Trokmê sit. The chieftain hissed when he saw his slaughtered comrades. Gerin waved at them and went on, "You and your friends heard the Sibyl's words, but did they heed them? Not a bit, and see what's become of them now. Sure as sure the same'll befall you and your clansmen if you go following Balamung's war-trumpets. Should I give

94

you your life, would you go and tell them that, aye, and others you meet on your way?''

Divico's red brows came together as he thought. At last he said, "Fox, I like you not, but I will. By Taranis, Teutates, and Esus I swear it." That was the strongest oath the Trokmoi knew: if it would not bind him to his word, nothing would.

"Good man!" Gerin said, clasping his hand and helping him to his feet. He almost told the Trokmê he thought like an Elabonian, but judged the proud chieftan would think it an insult.

"A moment," Etchebar said dryly. "You have not the only claim on this man. Because of him blood was shed in the holy precinct, which is abhorrent to our lord Biton." He touched his eyes and the back of his head in reverance. Falfarun nodded vigorous agreement. The guardsmen leveled their spears at Divico, who shrugged and relaxed but kept his hand near his sword.

"I am sure we can come to some sort of understanding," Gerin said, propelling the guard captain and priest into a quiet corner. There they argued for some minutes. The Fox reminded them the Divico had opposed Catuvolcus, who had started the unholy combat. Furthermore, he pointed out, Biton was quite capable of dealing with those who offended him, as he had proved on the thief whose luckless body was displayed in the forecourt. Etchebar growled a curt order and Divico was set free. The Trokmê bowed to Gerin and left, one hand still clutched to his aching skull.

Black-robed temple servitors dragged away the dead Trokmoi and began to mop up their spilled gore, which had already attracted a few droning flies. Eyes still unhappy under bushy eyebrows,

95

Etchebar gathered up his men and led them back to the forecourt. "And now, gentles, to the Sibyl at last," Falfarun said, with quite as much solemn aplomb as he had had before he was tossed about and his gleaming robe befouled.

The mouth of the Sibyl's cave was a black, grinning slit. Elise, still wan, took Gerin's hand; looking down into the inky unknown, he was glad of its pressure. Van fumed blasphemously as he tried to scrub sticky drying blood from his corselet. Falfarun vanished down the cavemouth. "You need have no fear for your footing," he called. "Since the unhappy day a century ago when the cousin of the Emperor Forenz (the second of that name, I believe) tumbled and broke an ankle, it was thought wise to construct regular steps and flooring to replace dirt and rocks. Such is life," he sighed, a bit unhappy at tradition flouted.

The subterranean corridor to the Sibyl's cave went down and down, twisting until Gerin lost all idea of the direction of his travel. A few dim candles set in brackets of immemorial antiquity gave a pale and fitful light; in it the flapping shadow of Falfarun's robe was a monstrous thing. Cross-branches of the caverns were holes of deeper blackness in the gloom. Elise's grip on Gerin's hand tightened.

Most of the cavewall was left in its natural state, and now and again a bit of rock crystal would gleam for a moment in the candlelight and then fade. A few stretches were walled off by brickwork of a most antique mode.

When Gerin asked the reason for the brickwork, Falfarun answered with a shiver. He said, "behind

96

the bricks are charms of great fellness, for not all the branches of these caves are safe for men. As you have seen, some we use for armories, others to store grain or treasure. But in some branches dread things dwell, and those who tried to explore them never returned. Those ways were stopped, as you see, to prevent such tragedies. More than that I cannot tell you, for it was done ages ago.''

Imagining the pallid monsters that could inhabit such dismal gloom, Gerin shivered himself. He tried not to think of the tons of rock and earth over his head. Van muttered something which might have been prayer or curse and hitched his swordbelt higher on his hip.

An ancient statue of Biton smiled its secret smile at them as they neared the Sibyl. The candles gave way to brighter torches, and the corridor widened to form a small chamber. A gust of cool, damp wind blew past Gerin's face, and heard the deep mutter of a great Stygian river far below. He started when Falfarun touched his elbow. ''Your gifts entitle you to privacy with the Sibyl, if such is your desire,'' the priest said.

Gerin thought, then nodded.

Surprisingly, Falfarun's bruised face crinkled into a half-smile. ''Good,'' he said. ''Did the answer you received please you not, belike your brawny friend would undertake to pitch me through a wall.'' Van sputtered in embarrassment. Falfarun went on, ''Good fortune attend you, gentles, and I leave you with the Sibyl.'' He waved at the throne set against the rear wall of the chamber and was gone.

''By my sword,'' Van said softly, ''if I didn't know better I'd say it was carved from one black pearl.'' Taller than a man, the high seat glimmered nacreously in the torchlight, crowns of silver shining on its two back posts.

The throne's splendor made the bundle of rags sitting upon it almost invisible. Though the Trokmoi had called the Sibyl a crone, Gerin had not been able to believe the withered body through which the gods had spoken ten years before still held life. But it was she, one eye dim, the other whitened by cataract. Her face was a badlands of wrinkles; her scalp shone through thinning strands of yellowish hair.

The mind behind that ruined countenance was still sharp, though. She raised one withered claw in gesture of command. ''Step forward, lass, lads,'' she said, her voice a dry rustle. Gerin knew she would have called his father ''lad'' had it been him before her, and she would have been as right.

''What would you know of my master Biton?'' she asked.

For some days Gerin had been mulling over the question he would put. Still, in that place his tongue stumbled as he asked, ''How best may I save myself and my lands and destroy the wizard who threatens them?''

Thinking she had not heard, the baron opened his mouth to ask his question once more. But with no warning, her eyes rolled back, showing only vein-tracked whites. Her scrawny fists clenched; her body shook and trembled, throwing her robe off one dry shoulder and revealing an empty dug. Her face twisted, and when she spoke it was not in her own voice, but that of a powerful man in the first flush of his strength. Hearing the god, Gerin and his companions went to their knees as his

98

words washed over them:
"Buildings fall in flame and fire:
Against you even gods conspire.
Bow before the mage of the north
When all his power is put forth
To crush you down, to lay you low:
For his grave no man will know."
The god's voice and power gone, the Sibyl slumped forward in a faint.

chapter 5

Evening came with gray clouds scudding across the sky and the wet-dust smell of rain in the air. Grim and silent, Gerin began to help Van make camp. Elise, worry in her voice and on her face, said, "Not three words have you said since we left the temple."

All the rage and helplessness the baron had confined since he stalked frozen-faced past Falfarun to reclaim the wagon came boiling up now in a torrent of bile. He slammed his helmet to the ground; it rolled spinning into the undergrowth. "What difference does it make?" he demanded bitterly. "I might as well cut my own throat and save that perambulating corpse the work. The Sibyl told me just what he did, though from him I hadn't believed it. I was a fool to go to her; advice is what I wanted, not a death sentence. A plague take all oracles!"

At that Van looked up. While Gerin was storming he had quietly gone on with the business of setting up camp, starting a fire and draining the blood of a purchased fowl into a trench to propitiate the ghosts. "I knew a man who said something like that once, Captain," he said.

"Is there a story to go with the knowing?" Elise asked, seemingly searching for any means to draw Gerin out of his inner darkness.

"Aye, so there is," Van agreed. He understood well enough what she was after, and pitched his words toward the Fox. Elise settled herself by the fire to listen. "Captain, you know—or you've heard me say—the world is round, no matter what any priest may blabber. I know. I should; I've been all the way around it. Maybe ten years back, it was, when I was at the far eastern edge of this continent, that I hired on as a man-at-arms under a merchant named Zairin, who was moving a shipment of jade, silk, and spices from a place called Ban Yarang to Selat, a couple of hundred miles southeastward. The folk are funny round those parts, little yellow-skins with slanting eyes like the Shanda nomads. It looks better on the women, I must say. Still, that's no part of the yarn.

"Zairin was one of those people who has no truck with the gods. Now, in those parts it's a customary thing to check the omens by watching the way the sacred peacocks peck at grain. If they eat well, the journey will be a good one; if not, it's thought wiser to try again some other time.

"There we were, all ready to set out, and Zairin's right-hand man, a fat little fellow named Tzem, brought us a bird from the shrine. He poured out the grain, but the peacock, who probably hadn't much liked traveling slung under his arm for more than a mile, just looked at it. He wouldn't touch it for anything, not that bird.

"Zairin sat watching this, getting madder and madder. Finally the old bandit had himself a gut-

101

ful. He got up on his feet and roared out, 'If he won't eat, let him drink!' and, may my beard fall out if I lie, he picked up that peacock, chucked it into the Kemlong river (which runs through Ban Yarang) and started off regardless.''

Gerin was caught up in spite of himself. "Dyaus! It's not a chance I'd like to take," he said.

"And you the fellow who curses oracles? You can imagine what we were thinking, but most of the way things went well enough. The road was only a bare-dirt track through the thickest jungle I've ever seen, and we lost a couple of porters to venomous snakes the poor barefoot fools stepped on, and one more to a blood-sucking demon that left him no more than a withered husk when we foiund him the next morning. But when you make a trip like that, you learn to expect such things, and Zairin was mightily pleased with himself. He was always laughing and telling anyone who'd listen what a lot of twaddle it was to pay any attention to a fool bird.

"Well, it couldn't have been more than a day and a half before we would have made Selat and proved the old croaker right when everything came unraveled at once. A dam broke upstream from where we were fording a river and drowned five men and half our donkeys. The customs man Zairin knew at the border had been transferred, and I shudder to think of the silver his replacement gouged out of us. Half the men got a bloody flux; it bothered me for two years. And just to top everything off, old Zairin came down with the crabs. From then on, Captain, he was a believer, I can tell you!''

"Go howl!" Gerin said. "I was hoping you'd cheer me with a yarn where a prophesy was shown wrong. I know enough of the other sort myself. For that you can stand first watch."

"Can I, now? Well, *you* can—" the outlander scorched Gerin in more tongues than the Fox knew. Finally he said, "Captain, fair is fair: I'll wrestle you for it."

"Aren't you the bloodthirsty one? I thought you'd had enough fighting for one day," Gerin sighed, pulling off his tunic. He helped Van undo the leather laces of his back-and-breast; his friend sighed as the weight came off. In kilt and sandals Van seemed more a war-god than ever. As he stretched, his bulging thews rippled and flexed like crushing snakes and the forest of golden hair on his chest and belly flashed in the firelight. Only his scars told of his humanity and his turbulent past. One terrible gash ran right armpit to navel; every time he saw it, Gerin wondered how the outlander had lived.

Not that he was unmarked himself: sword, spear, knife and arrow had left their signatures on his skin, and the cut Viredorix had given him was not much more than half-healed. He saw Elise's eyes travel from Van's enormous frame to him and knew he seemed almost a stripling beside his mountainous companion, though he was a well-made man of better than average size. But the Fox had a name as a wrestler on both sides of the Niffet. He had learned more tricks from masters south of the Kirs than his neighbors had ever imagined, and thrown men much bigger than himself. For all that, though, Van's raw strength was enough to flatten him as often as he could finesse

103

his way to victory. When the word went out that they would tussle, even Trokmoi came to watch and bet.

Embarrassed that her look had been seen and understood, Elise dropped her eyes. Gerin grinned at her. "He won't chuck me through a tree, girl. At least, I hope he won't."

"Who says I won't?" Van bellowed, and charged like an avalanche. Gerin sprang to meet him. Ducking under the thick arms which would quickly have squeezed the breath from him, he hooked his own left arm behind Van's right knee and rammed a shoulder into his hard-muscled middle. Van grunted and went down, but a meaty paw dragged Gerin after him. They rolled, thrashed, and grappled in the dirt, but when the dust cleared Gerin rode Van's broad back, his arms slid under his friend's shoulders and hands clasped behind his neck. Van slapped the ground and Gerin let him up. He shook his head and rubbed his eye to rout out a speck of dust. "You'll have to show me that one again, Gerin," he said. "Another fall?"

The baron shrugged. "All right, but that last one was for the watch." Van nodded, and in mid-nod he leaped. There was no chance for Gerin to use any of his feints or traps; he was seized, lifted, and slammed to earth with rib-jarring force. Van sprang on him like a starving lion onto a fat sheep.

Thoroughly pinned, Gerin grumbled, "Get off me, you pile of suet!" Van snorted and pulled him to his feet. They both swore as they swabbed each other's scratches with beer-soaked rags; the stuff stung foully.

After supper Gerin began to regret not having the first watch. He was sure he was too full of troubles to sleep, despite the day's exertions. He tossed, wriggled until a small stone no longer gouged his back, wished the crickets were not so loud . . .

Van watched his friend's face relax as slumber overtook him. He was not too worried about the baron's dejection, for he had seen him downhearted before, and knew he recovered rapidly. But the Fox felt his responsibilities deeply; if anything, a menace to his lands hit him harder than a threat against himself.

More and more clouds blew in from the west, pale against the dark blue dome of the sky. Math, a day past first quarter, and mottled Tiwaz, now nearly full, jumped in and out of sight, and a couple of hours before midnight dim Nothos' waning gibbous disc joined them. The wind carried a faint salt tang from the Orynian Ocean far away. Van scrubbed dried gore from his armor and helm and patiently waited until it was time to wake Gerin.

Rain threatened all through the Fox's watch; it was still dark when the first spatters came. Elise jumped when a drop splashed her cheek; she woke as quickly and fully as any soldier. She smiled at Gerin and said, " 'The gods in the heaven send dripping-tressed rain/ To nourish sweet hope in a desert of pain'—or so the poet says, anyway.''

He stared at her. The passage of a night had eased much of his gloom; now sheer surprise banished the rest. ''Where did you learn to quote Lekapenos? And whose rendering is that? Whoever did it knew his Sithonian well.''

''As for the rendering,'' she shrugged, ''it's mine. That passage always appealed to me. Where

105

else would I learn my letters than from the epics?''

There was much truth in that. The baron still recalled the godlike feeling he'd had when the curious marks on parchment began to correspond with the verses he'd learned by ear.

He was glad to exchange the dirt road that led to Ikos for the main southbound highway before the former became a bottomless river of mud. Moments later he was wondering at the wisdom of his choice. Behind them came a drumming of hooves, the deadly clangor of bronze on bronze and wheels rumbling on stone roadbed—a squadron of chariotry, moving fast.

Van unshipped his spear and Gerin began to string his bow. Then a deep voice sounded above the rising clatter: ''Way! Way for the men of Aragis the archer!''

The baron pulled off the road with almost unseemly haste. Ignoring the rain, Aragis' hardbitten troopers pounded past, brave in surcoats of scarlet and silver. A handful of draggled bandits were their reluctant companions. Proud hawk-face never smiling, Aragis' captain—or perhaps it was Aragis himself—raised one arm in salute as his men thundered by. Some of them had leers for Elise, stares for Van's fine cuirass. The bandits looked stolidly ahead; Gerin guessed they could already see the headsman's axe looming across their futures, and precious little else.

''Whew!'' Van said as the chariots disappeared into the mist ahead. ''This trip will make a fine yarn, but it's not something I'd like to do more than once.''

''You could say that about most things that make good stories,'' Gerin pointed out. Van chuckled and agreed.

From Ikos to Cassat was a journey of two days. To the baron it was a time of revelation. For years his mind had not reached further than the harvest, the balance of a blade, or the best place to set an ambush. But Elise had read many of the works that were his own favorites and, better yet, thought on what she read. They passed hour after hour quoting favorite passages and arguing meanings. Gerin had almost forgotten there could be talk like this; over the years, all without his knowing it, his mind had grown stuffy and stale, and now he relished the fresh new breeze playing through it. Van chimed in too from time to time; he might lack the shared background of Gerin and Elise, but he had seen more of the varied ways of man than either, and his wit was keen.

Like most summer rains in the northlands, the storm lasted little more than a day. As the sky cleared the purple bulk of the High Kirs, a great rampart looming tall on the southern horizon dominated the landscape. Eternal snow clung to many peaks, scoffing at the high summer below. Eight passes traversed the mountains; seven the Empire had painstakingly blocked over the years to prevent the incursions of the northern barbarians, once so frequent. In the foothills before the eighth squatted the town of Cassat, a monument to what might have been.

Oren II had planned it as a splendid capital for the new province his father had won; its great central square was filled by temples, triumphal arches, law-courts, and a theater. But fate had not been kind. Birds nested under the eaves of the noble buildings, and grass pushed its way up be-

107

tween marble paving-blocks. The only reality to Cassat was its barracks, squat, unlovely structures of wood and grimy plaster, where a few hundred soldiers of the Imperium pretended to rule the northlands. A few streets full of horsetraders, swordsmiths, joyhouses, and grogshops tended to their needs. The dusty wind blew mournful through the rest of the town.

The dragon flag of the Empire, black on gold, flew only over the barracks. There did Carus Beo's son, the Marchwarden of the North, perform his office; mice alone disputed in the courthouse Oren had built. Carus had once been a favorite at court. He had earned his present post some years before, when the Urfa massacred a column he led. Because of what he saw as his exile to the cheerless north, he despised and resented the border barons. Gerin called on him nonetheless. Few as they were, Carus' men would be a valuable aid in holding the border against the Trokmoi, could he be persuaded to send them north. Elise accompanied the Fox; Van took the wagon to a leading seller of horseflesh, seeking fresh animals to replace Gerin's well-bred but weary beasts.

The Marchwarden of the North sat at a well-scuffed desk piled high with parchments of all sizes. He was sixty or even a few years past; his yellowish-white hair had retreated to a ruff round his ears and the back of his neck, leaving all his pink scalp bare save for a meager forelock. There were dark pockets under his eyes, and his jowls quivered when he lifted his head from whatever bureaucratic inconsequentiality Gerin's arrival had interrupted.

"My man tells me you seek the assistance of the

Empire against the Trokmoi. Surely the boldness of the brave holders of Elabon's frontier cannot have declined to such an abysmal level?'' he said, looking at Gerin with no liking at all. His narrow eyes swiveled to Elise, and a murky gleam lit them. There was a liking there, right enough, but only of the sort that tempted the Fox to kick his stained teeth down his throat. Elise studied a point on the wall directly behind Carus' forehead.

"Surely not," Gerin agreed, stifling his annoyance. Ignoring the fact that he had not been offered a seat, he handed Elise into a chair and took another for himself. Carus' sallow cheeks reddened in irritation. Just as if nothing had happened, the Fox resumed, "At the present time, however, circumstances are of unusual difficulty." He went on to tell the Marchwarden of Balamung and his threatened invasion.

Carus was drumming his nails on the desktop by the time the Fox finished. "Let me see if I understand you correctly," he said. "You expect the troops of the Empire to get you out of the trouble into which you have gotten yourself with this wizard, who, if I may speak frankly, does not strike me as being overwhelmingly dangerous. Now to justify this service, you may point to— what?''

"Among other things, that we border barons have kept the Trokmoi out of the Empire for two hundred years and more.''

"A trivium.'' Carus waved his hand in a languid southern gesture which might have seemed courtly on Rihwin but was grotesque coming from a man of the Marchwarden's years and corpulence. "If I had my way, we would merely send a few thousand

109

tons of stone down behind the Great Gate. That would quite nicely seal off the barbarians for all time.''

''Horseballs,'' Gerin muttered. Elise heard him and smiled, but Carus heard him too, and that the baron had not intended.

''Horseballs?'' Carus' mouth moved in what might have been a smile, but his eyes stayed cold. ''Ah, the vivid turn of phrase of the frontier. But do let me return to what I was saying: indeed, I think the Empire would be just as well without you. What do we gain from you? No metals, no grain: only trouble. Half the rebels of the past two hundred years have had northern ties. You corrupt the calm, orderly way of life we crave. No, my good lord Gerin, if the barbarians can eat you up, they are welcome to you.''

The Fox had not really expected much help from the Marchwarden, but he had not expected outright hatred, either. He drew in a long angry breath. Elise pressed his hand in warning, but he was too nettled to pay heed. He spoke in the same polished phrases Carus had used, and the same venom rode them. ''You complain the Empire has received nothing form us? Up on the border, *we* wonder what we get from *you*. Where are the men and chariots of the Empire, to help us drive away the northern raiders? Where are they when we fight among ourselves? Do you care? Not a bit, for if we are kept distracted, why then we cannot think of rebellion. You judge, and rightly, our flesh and blood a better shield than any you might make of stone or wood, and so we die, for nothing.''

Bowing to Carus, Gerin stood to go. ''And you, my fine Marchwarden, you have gained the most of all from our thankless toil, for while we sweat and bleed to keep the border safe, here you have stayed for the past twenty-five years, shuffling papers from one pile to the next and sitting on your fat fornicating fundament!'' The last was a roar of surprising volume.

Carus leaped to his feet, fumbling for a sword but finding only an empty scabbard. Gerin laughed mockingly. ''Guards!'' bleated the Marchwarden, and when the men appeared he gabbled, ''Clap this insolent lout in chains and cast him in the dungeon until he learns politeness.'' His eyes lingered on Elise, and a flabby hand reached out to take her arm. ''I will undertake to instruct the wench personally.''

The expression of befuddlement on the guards' faces was ludicrous; they had not seen their master so active in years. Gerin made no move for his own blade. He said mildly, ''Do you know what will happen if you seize us? As soon as the barons learn of it, they will come down in a body and leave your precious barracks so much kindling, and not long after that the Trokmoi will be here to light it. It almost makes me sorry you won't live to see any of it.''

''What? What nonsense are you spewing now? I'll—*gark*!'' Carus' voice abruptly disappeared; Elise was tickling the soft skin under his wattled chin with the tip of her dagger. She smiled sweetly at him. The blood drained from his face, leaving it the color of the parchments on his desk. Moving very carefully, he detached his hold on her arm. ''Go,'' he said, in ragged parody of the pompous tones he had used moments before. ''Get out. Guards, take them away.''

111

"To the dungeons, sir?" asked one, scorn in his voice.

"No, no, just go." Carus sank back into his chair, hands shaking and beads of sweat gleaming on his bald pate. With as much ceremony as if it were a daily occurrence, his men conducted Gerin and Elise from the Marchwarden's rattled presence.

The sun was still high in the southwest; the audience had made up in heat what it lacked in length. Gerin turned to Elise and said, "I knew having you along would be a nuisance. Once he got a glimpse of you, the old lecher couldn't find a way to get me out of there fast enough."

"Don't be ridiculous. I'm a mess." Of itself, her hand moved to brush at her hair.

The baron surveyed her appreciatively. There was dust in her hair and a smudge of grime on her forehead, but her green eyes sparkled, the mild doses of sun she allowed herself had brought out a scattering of freckles on her nose and cheeks, her lips were soft and red, and even in tunic and trousers she was plainly no boy . . . easy there, he told himself. Do you want to make Ricolf your enemy too, along with the Trokmoi and Wolfar? He gave his beard a judicious tug. "You'll do," he said. "You'll definitely do."

She snorted and poked him in the ribs. He yelped and mimed a grab at her; she made as if to stab him. They were still smiling a half hour later when Van pulled up in the wagon. He smelled of horses and beer, and had two new beasts in the traces. A grin split his face. "Himself gave you the men, did he?" he asked eagerly.

"What? Oh. No, I'm afraid not." Gerin ex-

112

plained the fiasco; Van laughed loud and long. The Fox went on, "I expected nothing much, and got exactly that. You seem to have been pretty busy, though—what is that, anyway?" he jerked a thumb at one of Van's newly-acquired horses.

Unlike its companion, a handsome gray gelding, this rough-coated little beast was even less sightly than the shaggy woods-ponies of the Trokmoi. But Van looked scandalized; he leaped down and rubbed the animal's muzzle. A quick snap made him jerk his hand away, but he said, "Captain, don't tell me you don't know a Shanda horse when you see one? The fool trader who had him didn't. He thought he was putting one over on me. Well, let him laugh. A Shanda horse will run all day and all night; you can't wear one down if you try. I like the bargain, and you will too."

"All right, show me." Gerin helped Elise up, then climbed on himself. Van followed. The wagon clattered out of Cassat toward the Great Gate, the sole remaining link the Empire allowed itself with its northern province.

It was a long pull through the Gate. Toward the end of it the gray was lathered and blowing, but the horse from the plains showed no more sign of strain than if he had spent the day grazing. Gerin was impressed.

Though Elabon had not blocked this last way through the Kirs, her marshals had done their best to make sure no enemy could use it. A number of solid fortresses of brick and stone flanked the roadway. Watchmen trampled smartly along their battlements, alert against any mischance. The bronze-sheathed wooden gates of the towers were closed now, but could open to vomit forth chariots and footmen against any invader.

Wizards, too, aided in the defense of the Empire. They had their own dwellings, twin needle-like spires of what seemed to be multicolored glass, off which the late afternoon sun shimmered and sparkled. Should the armed might of the fortresses prove insufficient to blunt an attack, it was the duty of the warlocks to set in motion the thousands upon thousands of boulders heaped on either side of the pass, and thus block it forever. The arrangement made Gerin uneasy: what wizardry had made, it could easily unmake. He cheered slightly when he discovered the warriors in the fastnesses could also start the avalanches by purely natural means: there were paths leading up to the tops of the piles of scree, and certain triggering rocks there had levers under them. The Fox did not envy the fate of the men who would work them.

The succession of powerful strongholds awed even Van, who had only contempt for nations which relied on walls and garrisons for defense. "Folk who huddle in forts are dead inside," he said, "but with forts like these it will be a while yet before anyone notices the reek of the corpse."

Traffic through the Great Gate was heavy. There were traders heading north, their donkeys braying loud disgust at the weight of the packs they bore. There were traders coming south from their journeys, donkeys braying loud disgust over nothing at all. There were mercenaries, wandering wise men, wizards, and a good many travelers who fell into no neat scheme.

Nearly two hours went by before the wagon reached the end of the pass. Golden under the light

114

of the setting sun, the southern land spread out below like a landscape from a master painter's brush. Field and forest, town and orchard all were plain to see, and brooks and rivers were lines of molten copper.

"It's a rare pretty country," Van said. "What are the people like?"

"People," Gerin shrugged.

"I'd best keep an eye on my wallet, then."

"Go howl! You'd bite a coin free-given."

"Likely I would, if I planned to spend it."

"Scoffer!" Just then a warm, dry breeze wafted up from the south. It was sweet and spicy, with the faintest tang of salt from the distant Inner Sea, and carried scents the baron had forgotten. Like the frothing flow of a swift stream breaching the dam which had restrained it, long-buried memories flooded up in Gerin. He thought of the two years free from care he had spent in the City, and then of the sterile, worry-filled time since, and was appalled. "Why did I ever leave you?" he cried to the waiting land below. "Father Dyaus, you know I would sooner have been a starving schoolmaster in the City than King of all the Northlands!"

"If that is the way you feel, why not stay in the City?" Elise asked. Her voice was gentle, for the sight of the fair land ahead had enchanted her quite as much as the Fox.

"Why indeed?" Gerin said, surprised. He realized the notion had never crossed his mind before, and wondered why. At last he sighed and shook hs head. "Were the danger behind me less great, I'd leap at the chance like a starving long-tooth. But for better or worse, my life is on the cooler side of the mountains, and much depends on me there. If I stay, I would betray more than my own men. All the land will fall under Balamung's foul sorceries, and his evil thirst will not be slaked by it. It may happen yet; the gods have given the northland little enough hope. It is partly my fault that Balamung is what he is, and if I can make amends, I will."

"I think you will do well," Elise said slowly. "Often it seems the most glory is won by those who seek it least."

"Glory? If I can stay alive and free without it, I don't give a moldy loaf of journeybread for glory. I leave all that to Van."

"Ha!" Van said. "Do you want to know the real reason he's bound to go back, my lady?"

"Tell *me,*" Gerin suggested, curious to see what slander his friend would come up with.

"Captain, it would take more than a wizard to drive you away from your books, and you know it as well as I do." There was enough truth in that to make Gerin throw a lazy punch at Van, who ducked. Most of the spare silver the barony produced flowed south to the copyists and book-dealers of the City.

They wound their way down from the pass, hoping to reach a town before the sun disappeared. Gerin was less concerned about the ghosts than he would have been on the other side of the mountains; peace had reigned here for many years, and the spirits were relatively mild. For his part, Van grew downright eloquent when it came to the advantages of fresh food, a mug of ale (or even wine!), a comfortable bed, and perhaps (though he did not say so) a wench to warm it.

The road was flanked by a grove of fruit-trees of a kind unknown north of the Kirs. Not very tall, they had gray-brown bark, shiny, light green leaves, and were full of egg-shaped yellow fruit. Both leaves and fruit were fragrant, but Gerin remembered how astonishingly sour the fruit was to the tongue. It was called . . . he snapped his fingers in annoyance. He had forgotten the very name.

As the trees began to thin, another smell made its presence known through their perfume: a faint carrion reek. Gerin's lips drew back in a mirthless grimace; he knew too well what would be ahead. "I think we've found our town," he said.

The road turned, the screen of trees disappeared, and the town was there, sure enough. It was not big enough to have a wall, and the Fox was sure folk living ten miles from it had never heard its name. Nonetheless, it aspired to cityhood in a way open to the meanest of hamlets: by the road stood a row of crucifixes, each with its slow-rotting burden. Under them children played, now and then shying a stone upwards. Dogs slunk there too, dogs with poor masters or none, hoping for an easy meal.

Some of the spiked and roped victims were not yet dead. Through sun-baked and blistered lips they begged for water or death, each according to the strength left in him. One, newly elevated or preternaturally strong, still howled defiance at gods and men. His roars annoyed a few of the carrion birds nearby. Strong black bills filled with noisome food, they flapped lazily into the sky, feathered corruption staring down with fine impartiality on town, travelers, and field. They

117

knew all would come to them in good time.

Vans face might have been carved from stone as he surveyed the wretches overhead. Elise was pale and her eyes were wide with horror. Her lips shaped the word, "Why?" but no sound emerged. Gerin tried not to remember his own thoughts when he first encountered the malignant notions of justice the southerners had borrowed from Sithonia.

"Maybe," he said grimly, "I had my reasons for going home, after all."

chapter 6

The town (Gerin learned its name was Fibis) did little to restore the luster of the southlands in the baron's eyes. The houses lining the imperial highway were little if at all finer than the huts of his peasants, and only muddy alleys ankle-deep in slops led away from it. The sole hostel Fibis boasted was of a piece with the rest, being low-roofed, dingy, and small. The sign outside it had faded past legibility, and within the smell of old grease fought with but could not overcome the odors of rotting offal, urine from the dyeworks next door, and the never-absent stench from the crosses outside of town.

And the townsfolk! City ways which had seemed sophisticated to the youth who traveled this road ten years before were now either foppish or surly. Gerin tried to strike up a conversation with the innkeeper, a dour, weathered old codger named Grizzard, but got only inarticulate grunts in return. Giving up, he returned to the rickety table where his friends awaited supper. "If I didn't know better," he said, "I'd take oath the fellow is afraid of me."

119

"Then he thinks you've tasted his wine already," said Van, who was on his third mug. "What slop!" He swigged, pursed his lips to spit, but swallowed instead.

The rest of the meal was not much better. Plainly the lack of competition was all that kept Grizzard in business. Disgusted with the long, fruitless day he had put in, Gerin was about to head for his bed when a cheery voice said, "Hello, you're new here! What's old Grizzard given you to drink?" Without so much as a by-your-leave, the fellow pulled up a chair and joined them. He sniffed at their wine, grimaced, and flipped a spinning silver disc to the innkeeper, who made it disappear. "You can do better than this, you thief," he said. Much to the Fox's surprise, Grizzard could.

The baron studied his new acquaintance curiously, for the man seemed to be made of pieces which did not belong together. Despite his heartiness, his voice soon dropped so low Grizzard could not hear what he said, and while his mouth was full of slang from the City, his homespun tunic and trousers were rustic in the extreme. Yet his chin sported a gray imperial and his shoes turned up at the toe: both Sithonian styles. The name he gave—just Tevis, without patronymic or sobriquet—was one of the three or four commonest south of the moutains.

Whoever he was, he had a rare skill with words. Softly, easily, he enticed from Gerin (usually as close-mouthed as any man alive) the story of his travels, and all without revealing a bit of his own purpose. It was almost as if he cast a spell. He paused a while in silent consideration, his clear

120

dark eyes studying the Fox. "You have not been well-used by the Empire," he said at last.

Gerin only shrugged. His caution had returned, and he was wary of this smooth-talking man of mystery. Tevis nodded as if he had expected nothing more. "Tell me," he said, "do you know of Moribar the Magnificent, his Imperial Majesty's governor at Kortys?"

Van, who had drunk deep, stared at Tevis in owlish incomprehension. Elise was nearly asleep, her head warm on Gerin's shoulder. Her hair tickled his cheek and the scent of it filled his nose. But in his mind the stench of the rood was stronger still. Here was the very thing Carus Beo's son had feared most: a potential rebel in the capital of Sithonia seeking northern help. At any time but this the baron would have shed no tears to see the Empire go up in civil war, but now he needed whatever strength he could find at his back. He chose his words with care: "Tevis, I don't know you, and I didn't ask to know you. If you say one more word to me, you will have spoken treason, and I will not hear it. True, I've had my quarrels with some of his Majesty's servants, but if he does not plot against me in my land, I have no right to plot against him in his. I would not have drunk with you had I known what was in your mind. Here, take this and go." He laid a coin on the table to pay for the jug of wine.

Tevis smiled faintly. "Keep it," he said, "and this as well." He took something from the pouch at his belt, tossed it next to the coin, and was gone into the night while Gerin was still gaping at what he had thrown: a tiny bronze hand, fingers beginning to curl into a fist.

"Oh, great Dyaus above!" he said. "An Imperial Hand!" He propped his chin on his palm and stared at the little token before him. He could have been no more startled had it sprung up and slapped him in the face.

Bristles rasped under Van's fingers as he scratched his jaw. "And what in the five hells might that be?" he asked with ponderous patience.

"A secret agent, spy, informer . . . call him what you will. That doesn't matter. But if I'd shown any interest in setting Moribar on the throne, by this time tomorrow we'd be on crosses side by side, waiting for the vultures to pick out our eyes."

"Ha! I'd bite off their heads!" Van seemed more concerned with the vultures than the crucifixion that would invite them.

"That's one way of dealing with them, I suppose," Gerin agreed mildly. He woke Elise; she yawned and walked sleepily to the one room Grizzard grudged female travelers. Van and Gerin headed for their own pallets, hoping they would not be bug-ridden. Almost as an afterthought, the Fox scooped up the diminutive but deadly emblem Trevis had left behind.

Though weary, he slept poorly. The quarrel with Carus, his jarring reintroduction to the dark side of the southlands, and above all the brush with disaster in the shape of Trevis kept him tossing all night. The bed was hard and lumpy, too, and when he awoke half a dozen red, itchy spots on his arms and chest proved he had not slept alone.

Van was unusually quiet at breakfast. "Head hurt?" Gerin asked as they walked to the stables.

"What? Oh. No, it's not that, Captain."

Van hesitated. Finally he said, "I'll tell you right out, Gerin, last night I almost decided to buy myself a gig and get the blazes out of this crazy country."

Gerin had envisioned disaster piled on disaster, but not in his worst nightmares had he imagined his friend thinking of leaving. Ever since Van came to Fox Keep the two of them had been inseparable, fighting back to back and then carousing and yarning far into the night. Each owed the other is life more times than he would count. With a shock, the baron realized Van was a larger, gustier version of his dead brother Dagref. Losing him would have been far more than parting with a comrade; part of the baron's soul would have gone with him.

Before he could find a way to put any of what he felt into words, Elise spoke first, asking, "Why would you want to leave now? Are you afraid? The danger is in the north, not here." She seemed unwilling to believe her ears.

At any other time the outlander's wrath would have kindled had his courage been questioned. Now he only sighed and kicked at the pebble. There was genuine distress in his voice as he answered, "My lady, look about you." His wave encompassed not just the grubby little hamlet of Fibis and the crosses outside it, but all the land where the writ of the Empire was law. "You've seen enough of me in the past few days to know what I am and what my pleasures are: fighting, talking, drinking, aye and wenching too, I'll not deny. But here, what good am I? If I break wind in the backhouse, I have to look over my shoulder lest some listening spy call it treason. It's not the

123

kind of life I like to lead: worrying before I move, not daring even to think.''

Gerin understood that well enough, for much the same sense of oppression weighed on him. But Van was still talking: ''I was all set to take my leave of you this morning—head north again, I suppose. But then I got to thinking''—he suddenly grinned—'' and I decided if any boy-loving Imperial Hand doesn't like the way I speak, why, I'll carve the son of a pimp into steaks and leave him by the side of the road to warn his scurvy cousins!'' Elise laughed in delight and kissed him on the cheek.

''I think you planned this whole thing just to get that kiss,'' Gerin accused. ''Come on, you hulk, quit holding up the works.''

''Bastard,'' Van said, still grinning, and pitched his gear into the wagon.

The morning was still young when they splashed through the chilly Langros river. Though not as great as the Niffet or the mighty Charastos, which watered much of the plain of Elabon, its cold current ran swift as it leaped down from the Kirs toward the Greater Inner Sea.

The water at the ford was fairly high. It swirled icily around Gerin's toes and welled up between the wagon's floorboards. Most of the travelers' belongings were safe in sacks of oiled leather, but half the journeybread turned to slimy brown paste. Gerin swore in disgust, but Van said, ''Cheer up, Captain, the stuff wasn't worth eating anyhow.''

When they stopped to rest and eat, Van turned to Gerin and said quietly, ''Thanks for not pushing me this morning. You might have made it hard for me to stay.''

124

"I know," Gerin nodded, and neither of them mentioned the matter again.

They made good progress that day, passing small farms in the foothills, and then, as the land began to level out, going by great estates with splendid manor-houses set well back from the road. When shadows lengthened and cool evening breezes began to blow, by unspoken common consent they camped by the roadside instead of seeking an inn. Gerin fed and watered the horses as the sun set. In the growing darkness the ghosts appeared, but their wails were somehow muted, their cries almost croons.

Elleb's thin crescent soon followed the sun, like a small boy staying close to his father. That left the sky to the stars and Math, whose gibbous disc bathed the land beyond the reach of the campfire in a pale golden glow. As the night went on, she was joined by Tiwaz, whose speedy flight through the heavens had taken him well past full. And, when Gerin's watch was nearly done, Nothos poked his slow-moving head over the horizon. The baron watched him climb for most of an hour, then gave the night to Van.

The next day gave every promise of rolling along as smoothly as had its predecessor. The promise was abruptly broken a bit before noon. One of the manor-holders had decided to send his geese to market, and the road was jammed by an endless army of tall white birds herded along by a dozen or so men with sticks. The geese honked, cackled, squabbled, and tried to sneak off the road for a mouthful of grain. They did everything, in fact, but hurry. When Gerin asked their warders to clear a way so he could pass, they declined. "If these

125

blame birds get into the fields," one said, "we'll be three days getting them all out again, and our lord'll have our heads."

"Let's charge right on through," Van suggested. "Can't you just see the feathers fly?"

The very thought of a goose stampede brought a smile to Gerin's lips, but he said, "No, these poor fellows have their job to do too, I suppose." And so they fretted and fumed while the birds dawdled along in front of them. More traffic piled up behind. As time dragged on, Van's direct approach began to look better and better. The whip twitched in Gerin's hand. But before he used it he noticed the road was coming to a fork; the geese streamed down the eastern path. "Can we use the western branch to get to the City?" he called.

"You can that," one of the flock-tenders answered, and so the Fox swung the wagon down the new way.

New? Hardly. Gerin noticed that none of the others stalled behind the geese used the clear road, and soon enough found out why. The eastern branch of the highway was far newer, and after it was complete no-one had ever thought of the other one again. The wagon jounced and rattled as it banged over gaping holes in the road. On one stretch the paved surface vanished altogether. There the blocks had been set, not in concrete, but in molten lead. Locals had carried away blocks and valuable mortar alike once imperial inspectors no longer bothered to protect them. The baron cursed the lout who had sent him down this road and hoped he could make it without breaking a wheel.

The district had perhaps once been prosperous,

but when its road was superseded it decayed. More than one abandoned farmhouse was visible through the scrubby trees springing up everywhere in wheatfields no longer worked. The farther they went the thicker the forest grew, until at last its arms clasped above the roadway and squirrels flirted their gray bushy tails directly overhead. It would not be long until the very memory of the road was gone.

Finding a village in the midst of such decline seemed nothing less than divine intervention. Its inhabitants fell on Gerin and his friends like long-lost relatives, plying them with food and a rough, heady country wine and listening eagerly to every word they brought of the world outside. Not a copper would they take in payment. The baron blessed such kindly folk, and blessed them doubly when they confirmed that the road did in fact lead eventually to the City instead of sinking into a bog. "You see, Captain? You worry too much," Van said. "Everything will work out all right."

Gerin did not answer. He could not *let* things work out all right—he had to *make* them do so. Backtracking would have cost him a day he could not afford to spend.

The villagers insisted on putting up their guests for the night. Gerin's host was a lean farmer named Badoc son of Tevis (the baron hid a shiver). Other villagers, just as anxious for news, claimed Elise and Van.

The benches round Badoc's table were filled to overflowing by the farmer, his plump, friendly wife Leunadra, the Fox, and a swarm of children. These ranged in age from a boy barely able to toddle on up to Badoc's twin daughters Callis and

127

Elminda, who were about seventeen. They were striking girls, and Gerin eyed them appreciatively. They had dark, curly hair, sparkling brown eyes, and cheeks rosy under sun-bestowed bronze; their thin linen tunics clung to young breasts. As subtly as he could, the baron turned the conversation in their direction. They hung on his every word . . . so long as he was talking about Van. To his own charms they remained sublimely indifferent.

"I wish your friend could stay here," mourned one of the twins; Gerin had forgotten which was which. They both babbled on about Van's thews, his armor, his rugged features, his smile . . . and on and on, until Gerin began to hate the sound of his comrade's name. Badoc's craggy face almost smiled as he watched his guest's discomfiture.

At last the ordeal was over and the baron, quite alone and by then glad of it, went to his bed. His feet hung over the end, for Badoc had ousted one of his younger sons to accomodate the Fox. Gerin was tired enough that it fazed him not a bit.

It must have been around midnight when a woman's cry woke him. It was followed by another and then another, long and drawn out: *"Evoi! Evoiii!"* The baron relaxed; it was only the followers of Mavrix, the Sithonian god of wine, out on one of their moonlight revels. Gerin was a bit surprised the cult of Mavrix had spread to this out-of-the-way place, but what of it? He went back to sleep.

The next morning he discoverd the considerate villagers had not only curried his horses until their coats gleamed, but also had left gifts of fresh bread, wine, cheese, onions, and bars of dried fruit and meat in the back of the wagon. A troop of small boys followed him south until their parents finally called them home.

"I almost hate to leave," Van said. Gerin studied him: was the outlander still wearing the traces of a satisfied grin? What if he is, witling? the baron asked himself. Do you begrudge him his good fortune? Well, yes, a little, his inner voice answered.

The road was a bit better south of the village; at least it never disappeared. Under the trees the air was cool and moist, the sunlight subdued; Gerin felt more at home than he had since leaving Ricolf's keep. He was not alone; he heard Elise softly humming a song of the north-country. She smiled as she saw him watching her.

They came to a clearing almost wide enough to be called a meadow, hidden away deep within the forest. The Fox squinted at the sudden brightness. A doe which had been nibbling at the soft grass growing by the forest's edge lifted its head in horror at the wagon's noisy arrival and sprang into the woods.

"Pull over, would you?" Van asked Gerin. The outlander reached for Gerins bow and quiver. Though he disdained archery in battle, he loved to hunt and was a fine shot. He trotted across the clearing and vanished among the trees with grace and silence a hunting cat might have envied.

With a sigh, Gerin threw down the reins and stretched out full-length on the sweet-smelling grass, feeling sore muscles beginning to unkink. Elise stepped down and joined him. The horses were as glad at the break as the humans; they cropped the turf with as much alacrity as the deer

129

had shown.

Minute followed minute, but there was no sign of Van returning. "He's probably forgotten which end of the arrow goes first," Gerin said. He rose, went to the wagon, and emerged with Van's spear. Hefting it, he said, "Carrying this, I shouldn't wonder." Every time he touched it he marveled at his friend's consummate skill with such a heavy weapon.

He practiced slow thrusts and parries to while away the time, more than a little conscious of Elise's eyes on him. Showing off in front of a pretty girl was a pleasure which did not come his way often enough. More and more he resented the wound that had prevented him from courting this particular pretty girl. It was not that he lacked for women; if nothing else, a baron's prerogatives were enough to prevent that, though he was moderate in his enjoyment of them and never bedded a wench unwilling. But none of his partners had roused more than his lusts, and he quickly tired of each new liaison. In Elise he was beginning to suspect something he had thought rare to the point of non-existence: a kindred soul.

He had just dispatched another imaginary foe when a crackle in the bushes on the far side of the clearing made him raise his head. Van back at last, he thought and filled his lungs to shout a greeting. It froze, unuttered. Only a thin whisper emerged, and that directed at Ricolf's daughter: "Do just what I tell you. Walk very slowly to the far side of the wagon and then run for the woods. Move!" he snapped as she hesitated. He made sure she was on her way before loping into the middle of the clearing to confront the aurochs.

It was a bull, a great roan, its shaggy shoulder higher than the top of a tall man's head. Scars old and new crisscrossed its hide. Its right horn was a shattered ruin, broken off in some combat or accident long ago. The other curved out and forward, a glittering spear of death. The aurochs' ears twitched as it stared at the puny man who dared challenge it. The certainty of a charge lay like a lump of ice in Gerin's belly: any aurochs would attack man or beast, but a lone bull was doubly terrible. Drago's grandfather had died under the horns and stamping hooves of such a one.

Quicker ever than the Fox expected the charge came. The beast's hooves sent chunks of sod flying skyward. There was no time to throw Van's spear. All Gerin could do was hurl himself to his left, diving to the turf. He had a glimpse of a green eye filled with insane hatred and then the aurochs was past, the jagged stump of its horn shooting just over him. The rank smell of its skin fought the clean odors of grass and dirt.

Gerin was on his feet in an instant. But the aurochs was already wheeling for another charge, faster than any four-footed beast had a right to be. The Fox hurled his spear, but the cast was hurried and high. It flew over the aurochs' shoulder. Only a desperate leap saved Gerin. Had the bull two horns he surely would have been spitted. As it was, he knew he could not elude it much longer in the open.

He sprang up and sprinted for the forest, snatching up the spear as he ran. Behind him he heard the drumroll of the aurochs' hooves. The small of his back tingled, anticipating the thrust of

131

the horn. Then, breath sobbing in his throat, he was among the trees. Timber cracked as the aurochs smashed through brush and saplings. Still, it had to slow as it followed his dodges from tree to tree.

He had hoped to lose it in the woods, but it pursued him with a deadly patience he had never known any aurochs to show. Its bellows and snorts of rage rang loud in his ears. Deeper and deeper into the forest he ran, following a vague game trail.

That came to an abrupt end: sometime not long before, a forest giant had toppled, falling directly across the path. Its collapse had brought down other trees and walled off the trail as thoroughly as any work of man's might have done. Gerin clambered over the dead timber. The aurochs was not far behind.

The Fox's wits had been in a state of frozen dismay from the moment the aurochs had appeared in the clearing. They began to work again as he leaped down from the deadfall. Panting, "I can't run any farther anyway," he jabbed the bronze-clad butt of Van's spear deep into the soft earth, then blundered into the forest, having thrown his dice for the last time.

Even louder came the thunder of the aurochs' hooves, until the Fox could feel the ground shake. For a terrible moment he though it would try to batter through the dead trees, but it must have known that was beyond its power. Amazingly graceful, it hurled its bulk into the air, easily clearing the man-high barrier—and spitted itself on the upthrust lance.

At that impact the tough wood of the spearshaft

shivered into a thousand splinters, but the leaf-shaped bronze point was driven deep into the vitals of the aurochs. It staggered a couple of steps on rubbery legs blood spruting from its belly. Then a great gout poured from its mouth and nose. It shuddered and fell. Its sides heaved, then were still; it gave the Fox a reproachful brown bovine stare and died.

Gerin rubbed his eyes. In his dance with death out on the meadow he had been sure the beast's eyes were green. His hand came away bloody. He must have been swiped by a branch while dashing through the forest, but he had no memory of it. Shows how much I know, he thought, and wearily climbed back over the deadfall.

He had not gone far when Van came crashing down the game track, drawn bow in his hand. Elise was at his heels. The outlander skidded to a halt, his jaw dropping. "How are you, Captain?" he asked foolishly.

"Alive, very much to my own surprise."

"But—the aurochs . . . Elise said . . . " Van stopped, the picture of confusion. Gerin was glad Elise had had the sense to go after his friend instead of showing herself to the aurochs and probably getting herself killed.

"I'm afraid I'll have to buy you a new spear when we get to the City," Gerin said.

Van hauled himself over the barrier. He came back carrying the spearpoint; bronze was too valuable to leave. "What in the name of the trident of Shamadraka did you do?" he asked.

The baron wondered where Shamadraka's worshippers might live; he had never heard of the god. He explained in a few words. "Climbing

133

those trunks took everything I had left," he said. "The beast was hunting me like a hound—I've never heard of anything like it. He would have had me in a few minutes. But by some miracle I remembered a fable I read a long time ago about a slave who was too lazy to hunt. He'd block a trail, set a javelin behind his barrier, and wait for the deer to skewer themselves for him."

Elise said, "I know the fable you mean: the tale of the Deer and Mahee. In the end he's killed by his own spear, and a good thing, too. He was a cruel, wicked man."

"You got the idea for killing the brute out of a book?" Van asked, shaking his head. "Out of a *book?* Captain, I swear I'll never sneer at reading again, if it can show you something that'll save your neck. The real pity of it is, you'll never have a chance to brag about this."

"And why not?" Gerin had been looking forward to doing just that.

"Slaying a bull aurochs singlehanded with a spear? Don't be a fool, Gerin: who would believe you?"

Van had killed his doe while the baron battled the aurochs. He dumped the bled and gutted carcass into the wagon and uged the horses southward. None of the travelers had any desire to spend the night near the body of the slain monster. Not only would the corpse draw unwelcome scavengers, but its spilled blood was sure to lure hungry, lonely ghosts from far and wide, all eager to share the unexpected bounty of the kill.

When at length the failing light told them it was time to camp, the deer proved toothsome indeed. Van carved steaks from its flanks and they roasted

134

the meat over the fire. But despite a full belly the outlander was unhappy. He grumbled, "I feel naked without my spear. What will I do without it in a fight?"

Gerin was less than sympathetic. "Seeing that you've brought a mace, an axe, three knives—"

"Only two. The third is just for eating."

"My apologies. Two knives, then, and a sword so heavy I can hardly lift it, let alone swing it, I think you'll find some way to make a nuisance of yourself."

A nuisance Van was; he plucked a long straw from Elise's hand, leaving the short one—and the first watch—for Gerin. The Fox tried not to hear his friend's comfort-filled snores. His sense of the basic injustice of the universe was only slightly ameliorated when Elise decided not to fall asleep at once. Gerin was glad of her company. Without it, he probably would have dozed, for the night was almost silent. The sad murmurs of the ghosts, heard with the mind's ears rather than the body's, were also faint: the lure of the dead aurochs reached for miles, leaving the surrounding countryside all but bare of spirits.

For some reason the Fox could not fathom, Elise seemed to think him a hero because he had slain the aurochs. He felt more lucky than heroic; there was precious little glory involved in running like a rabbit, which was almost all he'd done. If he had not plucked what he needed from his rubbish-heap of a memory, the beast would have killed him. "Fool luck," he concluded.

"Nonsense," Elise said, "Don't make yourself less than you are. In the heat of the fight you were able to remember what you had to know and,

135

more, to put it into action. It takes more than muscle to make a hero.''

Not at all convinced, Gerin shrugged and changed the subject, asking Elise what she knew of her kin in the City. Her closest relative there, it transpired, was her mother's brother Valdabrun the Stout, who held some fairly high position at the Emperor's court. Though he did not say so, Gerin found that a dubious recommendation. His Imperial Majesty Hildor III was an indolent dandy, and there was scant reason to expect is coutiers to be different.

To hide his worry, he talked of the City and his own two years in it. Elise was a good audience, as city life of any sort was new to her. He told a couple of his better stories, and her laugh warmed the cool evening. She moved closer to him, eager to hear more.

He leaned over and kissed her. Looking back on it later, he often wondered just what had made him do it, but at the time it seemed the most natural thing in the world. For a moment her lips were startled and still under his, but then she returned the kiss, at first hesitantly, then with a warmth to match his own.

You do have a gift for complicating your life, he told himself as she snuggled her head into his shoulder. If things go on the way they've started, not only will Wolfar want to cut out your heart and eat it (a project he's been nursing quite a while in any event), but your old friend Ricolf will be convinced, note or no note, you ran off with his daughter for purposes having very little to do with taking her to her uncle. And what is she thinking? She's no peasant wench, to be honored by a

136

tumble and then forgotten. And further . . .

A plague on it all, he thought. He kissed her again.

But when his lips touched her soft white throat, she asked him softly, "Dear Gerin, was it for this, then, you decided to bring me to the City? Have I but traded one Wolfar for another?" She tried to keep her tone light, but hurt and disappointment were in her voice. They stopped him effectively as a dagger drawn, perhaps more so. She slipped free of his encircling arm.

He knew he had overstepped the bond of liking and sympathy growing up between them as they traveled. "I would never have you think that," he said.

"Nor do I, in truth," she replied, but the hurt was still there. The time to remember he was man and she maid might come later, he thought, or maybe not at all. It was not here yet, despite the cool quiet of the night and the moonlight filtering through the trees. They talked of inconsequential hings for a while, then she rose and walked to the wagon for her bedroll. As she passed him she stopped and her lips brushed his cheek.

Elleb's thick waxing crescent was well set and the nearly full Math, bright as a golden coin, beginning to wester when he woke Van and sank into exhausted slumber.

But then it was as if a strong gale arose within his sleeping mind and blew away the mists separating him from the country of his dreams.

Clear as if he had been standing on the spot, he saw the great watch-fires flame, heard the wild music of pipe, horn, and harp skirling up to the sky, saw the tall northern warriors gathered by the

137

fires, some with spears, others with drinking-horns in their hands. This is no common dream, he thought, and felt fear, but he could not leave it, not even when black wings drowned his sight in darkness.

These proved to be the flapping wings of the wizard's cloak Balamung wore. The gaunt sorcerer stepped back a pace, to be silhouetted against the firelight like a starving bird of prey. Only his eyes were live things, embers of scarlet and amber set in his skeletal face. The light played redly off his hollow cheeks. "Lord Gerin the Fox," he said, "it's nothing less than a nuisance you've been to me, nothing less, so I hope you'll be forgiving me if I cost you a dollop of sleep to show you what's awaiting in the northlands whilst you scuttle about the filthy south. Would I could be drawing the black-hearted soul of you right out of your carcass, but there's no spell I ken to do it, with you so far away and all."

Balamung called down curses on the Fox's head; he hoped they would not bite deep. On and on the wizard ranted, until he paused to draw breath and continued in a slightly calmer vein, saying, "Not least do I mislike you for costing me the soul of a fine fighting man this day. Like a wee bird I sent it flitting out, to light in the body of the great aurochs. Sure as sure I was he'd stomp you all to flinders and leave you a dead corp by the side of the road. Damn your tricky soul, how did you escape him? The soul of him died trapped in the beast, for I couldna draw it free in time, and when it flickered away, his body was forfeit too, puir wight."

No wonder the bull had trailed him with such

138

grim intensity! He likely had not been wrong when he thought its eyes were green, there in the meadow; that could well have been some byproduct of Balamung's magic. He had been lucky indeed.

"But sure and I'll have my revenge for him!" Balamung was screaming. Behind him the music had fallen silent. The spell the mage used must have been prepared beforehand, for when he cried out in the harsh Kizzuwatnan tongue a stout wicker cage rose from the ground and drifted slowly toward the fire. Gerin's spirit quailed when he saw it: he knew it was the custom of the Trokmoi to burn their criminals alive, and in this cage, too, a man struggled vainly to free himself.

"Die, traitor, die!" Balamung shouted, and all the gathered warriors took up the cry. Horror rose in Gerin, who suddenly recognized the condemned prisoner. It was Divico, the Trokmê chieftain whose life he had spared after the fight at Ikos. He wished sickly that he had let Van give the northerner a clean death. "Have a look at what befalls them that fight me," Balamung whispered, "for your turn is next!" His voice was cold as ice, harsh as stone.

While he was speaking, the cage entered the blaze. Some minor magic had proofed the wicker against the flame; no fire would hold on it. But wherever a tongue of it licked Divico it clung, flaring as brightly as if his body were a pitch-soaked torch. Held there by Balamung's wizardry, Gerin watched in dread as the flames boiled Divico's eyeballs in his head, melted his ears into shapeless lumps of meat that sagged and ran against his cheeks, then charred the flesh from those cheeks to leave the white bone staring through. Over the Trokmê's body the flames cavorted, but Balamung's evil magic would not let him die; he fought against the unyielding door until his very tendons burned away. His shrieks had stopped long before, when the fire swallowed his larynx.

"A job I had to rush, he was," Balamung said. "When it's you, now Fox, falling into my hands, I'll take the time to think of something truly worthy of you, oh indeed and I will!" He made a gesture of dismissal. Gerin found himself starting up from his bedroll, body wet with cold sweat.

"Bad dream, Captain?" Van asked.

Gerin's only answer was a grunt; he was too shaken for coherent speech. Divico's face being eaten by flames still stood before his eyes, almost more vivid than the dimly-lit campsite he really saw. He thought he would never want to sleep again, but his weary body needed rest more than his mind feared it.

The sounds of a scuffle woke him. Before he could do more than open his eyes, strong hands pinned him to the ground. It was still far from sunrise; did bandits in the southlands dare the darkness, or was this some new assault of Balamung's? He twisted, trying to lever himself up on an elbow and see who or what had overcome him.

"Be still, or I'll rend thee where thou liest." The voice was soft, tender, female, and altogether mad. More hands, all full of deranged strength, were pressing down his legs. They tugged warningly, and he felt his joints creak. All hope left him; having escaped Balamung's sorcerous forays,

140

it seemed unfair to die under the tearing hands of a band of the votaries of Mavrix. Why had the fertility god's orgiastic, frenzied cult ever spread outside his native Sithonia?

Moving very slowly, he turned his head about, trying to see the extent of the disaster. Perhaps one of his comrades had managed to get away. But no: in the moonlight he saw Van pinioned by more of the madwomen, his vast muscles twisting and knotting to no avail. Still more had fastened themselves to Elise.

The maenads' eyes reflected the light like those of so many wolves. That was the only light in them; there was nothing of human intelligence or mercy, for they were filled by the madness of the god. The finery in which they had begun their trek through the woods was ripped and tattered and splashed with mud and grime, their hair awry and full of twigs. One woman, plainly a lady of high station from the remnants of fine linen draped about her body, clutched the mangled corpse of some small animal to her bosom, crooning over and over, "My baby, my baby."

A blue light drifted out of the forest, a shining nimbus round a figure . . . godlike was the only word for it, Gerin thought. "What have we here?" the figure asked, voice deep and sweet like the drink the desert nomads brewed to keep off sleep.

"Mavrix!" the women breathed, their faces slack with ecstasy. Gerin felt their hands quiver and slip. He braced himself for a surge, but even as he tensed the god waved and the grip on him tightened again.

"What have we here?" Mavrix repeated.

Van gave a grunt of surprise. "How is it you speak my language?"

141

To the Fox it had been Elabonian. "He didn't —" the protest died half-spoken as his captors snarled.

The god made an airy, effeminate gesture. "We have our ways," he said . . . and suddenly there were two of him, standing side by side. They— he—gestured again, and there was only one.

As well as he could, Gerin studied Mavrix. The god wore fawnskin, soft and supple, and a wreath of grape leaves was round his brow. In his left hand he bore an ivy-tipped wand; at need, Gerin knew, it was a weapon more deadly than any mortal's spear. Mavrix's blond curls reached his shoulder, but his cheeks and chin were shaven. His soft-featured, smiling face was a pederast's dream, except for his eyes: two black pits reflecting nothing, giving back only the night. A faint odor of fermenting grapes and something else, a rank something Gerin could not name, floated up from him.

"That must be a useful art." The baron spoke in halting Sithonian, trying to pique the god's interest and gain at least a few extra minutes of life.

Mavrix turned his fathomless eyes on the Fox, but his face was still a smiling mask. He answered in the same tongue, "How pleasant to hear the true speech once more albeit in the mouth of a victim," and Gerin knew his doom.

"Are you in league with Balamung, then?" he growled, knowing nothing he said now could hurt him further.

"I, a friend to some fribbling barbarian charlatan? What care I for such things? But surely, friend mortal, you can see this is your fate. The madness of the Mavriad cannot, must not be

142

thwarted. Were it so, the festival would have no meaning, for what else is it but the ultimate negation of all the petty nonfulfillments of humdrum, everyday life?''

''It is not right!'' Elise burst out. ''Dying I can understand; everyone dies, soon or late. But after the baron Gerin'' —the Fox thought it a poor time for rhyming, but held his peace— ''singlehanded slew an aurochs, to die at the hands of lunatics, god-driven or no—''

Mavrix broke in, deep voice cracking. ''Who slew what?'' he demanded tensely.

Confused, Elise faltered, ''Gerin slew a great wild ox—''

Mavrix's smile gave way to an expression of purest horror. He screamed, filling the forest with the sound. ''The oxgoad come again!'' he wailed, ''but now in the shape of a man! Metokhites, I thought you slain!'' With a final despairing shriek, the god vanished into the depths of the wood. His followers fled after, afflicted by his terror—all but the lady of rank, who still sat contentedly, rocking her gruesome ''baby''.

Still surprised at being alive, Gerin slowly sat up. So did Elise and Van, both wearing bewildered expressions. ''What did I say?'' Elise asked.

Gerin thumped his forehead, trying to jar loose a memory. He had paid scant attention to Mavrix in the past, as the god's principal manifestations, wine and the grape, were rare north of the Kirs. ''I have it!'' he said at last, snapping his fingers. ''This Metokhites was a Sithonian prince long ago. Once he chased the god into the Lesser Inner Sea, beating him about the head with a metal-tipped oxgoad: Mavrix always was an arrant coward. I suppose he thought I was a new—what would the word be?—incarnation of his tormentor.''

"What happened to this Metokhites fellow?" Van asked. "It's not the smartest thing, tangling with gods.''

"As I remember, he chopped his son into bloody bits, being under the impression the lad was a grapevine.''

"A grapevine, you say? Well, Captain, if I ever seem to go all green and leafy-like, be so good as to warn me before you try to prune me.''

At that, the last of the maenads lifted her eyes from the ruined little body she dandled. There was a beginning of knowledge in her face, though she was not yet fully aware of herself or her surroundings. When she spoke, her voice had some of the authority of the Sibyl at Ikos: "Mock not Mavrix, lord of the sweet grape. Rest assured, you are not forgotten!" Gathering her rags about her, she swept imperiously into the woods, and silence fell on the camp.

The tribulations of Gerin the Fox, Van of the Strong Arm, and the Lady Elise have only just begun, as they draw nearer to the fabulous City of Elabon and the target of their quest, the Sorcerer's Collegium. Pursued by the curse of Mavrix as well as by the vengeful Balamung, the trio engage in even more fantastic and dangerous adventures in WERENIGHT, a Belmont Tower Book coming in April!